THE CHOSEN ONES:
A Sabina Kane Short Fiction Collection

JAYE WELLS

This is a work of fiction. Names, characters, places, and incidents are either the product of the author's imagination or are used fictitiously. Any resemblance to actual persons, places, or events is coincidental.

"Fool's Gold" © 2014 Jaye Wells
"Violet Tendencies" © 2011 Jaye Wells
"Rusted Veins" © 2013 Jaye Wells
"Fire Water" © 2015 Jaye Wells

Original cover designs by Wendy Chan
The Chosen Ones cover design by Jaye Wells

ISBN: 1545568545
ISBN-13: 978-1545568545

BY JAYE WELLS

The Prospero's War Series
Dirty Magic
Cursed Moon
Fire Water (novella)
Deadly Spells

The Sabina Kane Series
Red-Headed Stepchild
The Mage In Black
Violet Tendencies (short story)
Green-Eyed Demon
Silver-Tongued Devil
Blue-Blooded Vamp
Rusted Veins (novella)
Fool's Gold (novella)

Meridian Six Series
Meridian Six
Children of Ash

Other Works
The Uncanny Collection

Jaye Wells Writing as Kate Eden
The Hot Scot
Rebel Child

Table of Contents

Dear Reader,

In 2007, I was driving down the road one day when a bored voice said, "Digging graves is hell on a manicure." I didn't know it at the time, but that voice belonged to Sabina Kane, and that first introduction was the start of a beautiful friendship.

I completed the five-book Sabina Kane series in 2012. Writing that series was one of the greatest challenges of my life, but it was also one of the most rewarding. In addition to the main five novels, I also published one short story and two novellas. *Fool's Gold* was a prequel novella set in the 1970s in Los Angeles. It's the story of one of Sabina's early cases and gives the backstory on her relationship with Slade Corbin. *Violet Tendencies* was set between the novels *The Mage in Black* and *Green-Eyed Demon*, and it answers the question, "What happened to Valva?" Finally, *Rusted Veins* is a novella set in New Orleans during Halloween. It's set after the action of the main series arc, and follows Team Awesome as they track down a missing mage.

Until now, these three Sabina Kane stories have been available separately in ebook only. Because of distribution issues, the stories weren't available to readers in other countries. I also received lots of emails from readers asking for them in print. That's why I created this special print-only edition that compiles all the stories in one place. As a bonus, I've also thrown in a prequel novella for my Prospero's War series so you can meet my new friend Kate Prospero, too.

Revisiting these beloved characters for this collection has been sort of like attending a crazy family reunion. If you've never met these characters before, brace yourself for a wild ride. If you already know and love them, I know you'll enjoy yourself.

Happy reading!
Jaye Wells

FOOL'S GOLD

Los Angeles, November 1979

The guy on camera wore a ratty ski mask, a black turtleneck stretched precariously over a beer gut and too-tight bell-bottoms. The wall behind him was covered in some sort of collage done in shades of black and white with accents of red. I tried to make out the details, but the poor video quality made the picture fuzzy.

I shook my head at the grainy image. If it had been anyone else showing me this, I'd think it was a joke. But the Dominae weren't exactly known for their senses of humor. I glanced over at Slade. He wasn't smiling. He rarely did, from what I'd seen. Of course, I'd only known him for about ten minutes, and his lack of good humor was probably due to his not wanting to be saddled with a rookie.

"My name is Viper," the guy on tape said dramatically. I barely managed not to roll my eyes at the fake name. "For too long we, the mighty *Lilim*, children of Lilith, have hidden in the shadows. The time has come to reveal ourselves to the sons of Adam. Unless—"

He paused dramatically. I knew what was coming and resisted the urge to fast-forward through his lame speech.

"—the Dominae give me one billion dollars!"

I choked on a shocked laugh. Viper wasn't the first vampire to try to extort money out of the Dominae. But he was the first to demand such a ridiculous sum.

"The money must be deposited by midnight Wednesday or I will give all the major media outlets in LA the story of the century."

He went on to rattle off the name of a local bank and an account number. Tanith cut the tape off as he started to rant again.

"Do you have the envelope the tape came in?" Slade asked, all business. His look screamed badass assassin. Dressed in black from neck to toes, he wore a leather blazer, slacks, and expensive Italian leather shoes. In fact, the only things keeping his look from being a Shaft rip-off were his pale skin and auburn hair.

Tanith shook her head. Of the three Dominae who ruled the Lilim, she was in charge of the business side of running the race. Considering the sum of money this guy was demanding, it wasn't a surprise she was taking point on this. In all honesty, I was glad it was she and not my grandmother who was talking to us. As the Alpha of the race, Lavinia Kane rarely concerned herself with this sort of issue. But I was surprised she wasn't there to watch me squirm when Tanith told me my first job as an assassin would be shadowing someone. Disappointing me was somewhat of a hobby for my grandmother.

"We had them dusted," Tanith was saying. "No fingerprints."

Slade nodded. "Have you tracked the account he mentioned?"

"The account belongs to a Zeke Calebow." She slid a file across the table.

I scooted closer to Slade to get a look at the contents. He ignored me and focused on the papers. The picture clipped inside was a mug shot of a portly male vamp with shaggy copper hair and freckles. He looked stupid and mean—a bad combination. The guy in the video wore a ski mask, but my gut told me this Zeke and Lord Viper were one in the same.

"What do we know about Zeke?" I asked.

Tanith sighed. "Not much. Family is trash. Last known job was a strip club in the Valley."

Slade slammed the folder shut before I could read the name of the club from the dossier. "We'll check it out," he said in a clipped tone.

"You have seventy-two hours to neutralize this threat." Tanith said, looking from Slade to me and back again. "I don't think I have to remind you how sensitive this matter is. We want this guy dead yesterday."

"Consider it done," Slade said. Then he turned

on his heel and marched toward the door. He didn't look back to make sure I followed. But I did anyway.

∞

An hour later, Slade pulled up in front of the Tit Crypt. He hadn't said much to me on the way over. I tried to play it cool, but inside I was stoked. Even though I'd graduated with honors from assassin school five years earlier, most of my jobs thus far involved roughing up vampires who forgot to pay their tithes to the Dominae. This would be my first kill mission, which was why I'd been paired up with a more experienced assassin.

Among enforcers, Slade Corbin was a legend. The instructors at school spoke about his feats with reverence and had used some of his more daring missions as case studies. Rumor had it he was less than a century old, which was hard to believe. But looking at him, I believed it. The light auburn color gave him away. If he'd been an older vamp, the shade would be darker. For him to have accomplished so much at such a young age meant he was someone I'd be able to learn a few things from.

He turned the car off and leaned toward me. "Okay, this is how it's going to work. You're going to shut up and stay out of my way. I ask the questions. I make the decisions. And when we find this asshole, we're going to split the payment ninety-ten."

My mouth fell open. "Excuse me?"

"Which word didn't you understand?"

I cocked my head to the side. Slade might be a legend, but no one spoke to me that way. "Listen, buddy, I don't know who the hell you think you are, but the Dominae asked us to team up on this. I'm not going to sit around and let you collect all the money." Or the respect, I amended silently. I'd waited too long for a real chance to prove myself to the Dominae as an assassin for this guy to get all the glory.

"No, you listen, sweetheart. You make trouble and I will end you. I've got a lot riding on this payday for some rookie to fuck it up for me. So, you'll march your ass in there and watch while I find our guy and get the job done. For your trouble, you'll walk away with ten percent. And I'm being generous here. Ten large for doing nothing is a good deal."

I could tell this asshole wasn't going to listen to reason. Fine, I decided. Let him believe I was just some inexperienced hack. "Okay, I'll tell you what. I'll let you do the talking in there if you agree to a seventy-thirty split."

He cursed under his breath, something about godsdamned stubborn females. "How about ninety-ten and I don't kick you off the case altogether?"

"You can't do that!"

"Watch me."

∞

The bouncer at the door waved us in. Slade swaggered ahead of me, and I followed along, glaring daggers at his back.

I'd been in this place before. Being an enforcer for the Dominae meant I had to experience the seedier sides of the vampire underworld on a regular basis. Strip clubs especially seemed to attract tithe-avoiding repeat offenders, so I spent a lot of time staking them out. That allowed me to make contacts with the club owners and bouncers, who understood the benefits of cooperating with an enforcer. For me, the relationships meant I had access to the who's who in order to find out the what's what.

As far as clubs went, the Tit Crypt fell into the lower end of the spectrum. Instead of valet service and tight-assed chicks with glorious racks, it offered an all-you-can-eat buffet and hard-looking females who didn't even try to conceal the boredom on their overly made-up faces.

On the stage, a female with red hair twisted into Bo Derek braids swayed her hips in time to the disco tragedy of Donna Summer's "Bad Girls." I shook my head at the music. How a race that had invented disco managed to rule the world while vampires had to stay in the shadows escaped me.

In contrast to the disco-inspired fashions favored by most of the strippers, I wore a "God Save the Queen" T-shirt studded with safety pins, torn jeans, and biker boots. I topped the entire ensemble off with a beaten leather jacket I'd found at Goodwill. The confrontational look discouraged the roving hands and eyes of the club patrons.

I continued past the stage and the interested stares of the men seated there. Fang, a male vamp with a mustache that would have made Burt Reynolds jealous, wiped the bar down with a dingy towel. He regarded Slade with mean, narrowed eyes as he approached. I hung back, as instructed, biding my time.

"I need some information." Slade slammed a twenty on the bar.

The rag slowed its circling as Fang turned unfriendly eyes on him. "Ain't got none for sale."

Slade sighed and slapped another twenty down, harder this time. "I'm looking for one of your employees."

Fang leaned forward. "Look, mister, you want to look at some titties, you've come to the right place. If you're asking me to squeal on my people, you'd best turn your ass around and go."

I choked on a laugh at the look on Slade's face. His jaw clenched, obviously a precursor to violence. I stepped out from behind the column I'd waited behind. The move drew Fang's attention.

His face transformed into a smile that flashed some fang. "Amateur night is on Tuesdays."

I grinned and strutted over the bar to run a finger down Fang's leather vest. "How about a private dance, then, hot stuff?"

Fang leaned his elbows on the bar. "You sure your boyfriend here won't mind, Sabina? From the glare he's sending me, his mama never taught him how to share."

"Don't mind him," I said, waving away Slade's fierce frown. "Listen, Fang, I was hoping you could help me out with something."

Fang's moustache twitched. "Anything for you, good-lookin'."

"We're looking for Zeke Calebow."

Fang frowned. "What you want with that lousy son of a bitch? I had to fire his ass."

"Why?"

"Bastard cut a peephole in the girls' dressing area. Caught him jacking off in the utility room with his eye glued to the wall." He shook his head. "Two of my best girls quit when they found out."

Slade spoke up. "Do you know where we can find him?"

Fang sent Slade a contemptuous look. "Last I heard, he took a job at T&A Video over on Victory."

"Yeah, I know the place."

"Did Zeke ever say anything antagonistic about the Dominae?" Slade asked.

I froze and held my breath while I waited for Fang's reaction.

The bald vampire threw his head back and laughed. "Shit, son, do you think this is one of them sacred temples to the Great Mother? Everyone around here says shit about the Dominae."

Slade pressed his lips together. "This isn't a joke," he snapped. "Do you think the Dominae send out two Enforcers to hunt down people to deliver a warning?"

Fang sobered quickly. "Look, if Zeke stepped in some shit, it's not my business. Like I said, he doesn't work here anymore."

"If you think of anything else that might help, will you call me?" I asked.

The vampire winked. "Sure thing, doll."

"Thanks, Fang," I said. "I appreciate it."

"I don't suppose you'd prefer to show your appreciation topless," he said with a twinkle in his eye.

I laughed and shook my head. "How about a rain check?" I slid an extra twenty across the bar. Fang pocketed the payment smoothly.

Fangs chuckled. "Yeah. I'll call you right after I beat his perverted ass."

Slade frowned at the vamp. "Just as long as you leave the killing to the professionals."

∞

Slade grabbed my arm and swung me around before I'd taken three steps out the door.

"You want to explain to me what the fuck you were thinking in there? I thought we'd agreed you'd let me do the talking."

I jerked my arm free of his grasp. "First of all, you're welcome for getting the information we needed. And second, Fang never would have talked to you if I hadn't been there."

"And why is that? You been doing some moonlighting?"

I crossed my arms. "The vamps who don't pay their tithes usually spend them on one of three things: gambling, titty bars, or prostitutes. I know just about every vamp bookie, club owner, and pimp in the city." I stepped up on Slade, emboldened by the small victory of shocking him. "And if you'd taken two seconds to ask me instead of issuing orders, I would have told you that there was no way Fang would talk to you."

"Why not?"

"Because Fang's brother was killed by an enforcer for bootlegging blood-wine during Prohibition."

"Why does he talk to you, then?"

"Because I flirt with him shamelessly." I smiled. "And because I saved one of his best girls from being raped by a patron several months ago. Fang loves his girls, and by helping one of them, he considers himself in my debt."

"Oh," Slade said.

"Yeah," I said. "And if you drop the asshole routine on the way to T&A Video, I'll tell you all about Larry Garrett, San Fernando Valley's vampire porn king."

∞

A small bell dinged over the door as Slade held it open and motioned for me to go first. He'd been surprisingly quiet after our little chat. I took that as a good sign, since he seemed the type who liked to bark orders unnecessarily. So, as I brushed past him, I was feeling good. At least until I caught a whiff of the store—a charming perfume of stale cigarettes, body odor, and dried semen.

T&A Video lay in the armpit of the San Fernando Valley. The introduction of VHS tapes a few years earlier had revolutionized the adult film industry, and T&A was just one of the many new establishments catering to the discerning wank-film connoisseur.

On the surface, it looked like your typical video store, except with sections dedicated to every fetish known to man—and sometimes beast. But in the back, it held one of the most extensive collections of vampire porn in Southern California.

As expected, Larry manned the counter. He

had an unlit cigar clamped between his lips and wore a polyester shirt covered in a retina-burning psychedelic print. I thought the thick chain with the male symbol was a nice touch, though. Over Larry's head, a TV bolted to the ceiling displayed a scene involving a pizza deliveryman and a woman whose undercarriage looked like one of *Star Trek*'s tribbles.

Near the back of the store, a clean-cut businessman perused shelves labeled "Barely Legal." If he'd seen me come in, he was doing a pretty good job pretending he hadn't. He pulled a video from the shelf and added it to the three he was already holding.

A red curtain next to the checkout was drawn back and a young guy exited. His hand was busy zipping his fly when he noticed me. His cheeks went red and he scuttled by so fast, he left a breeze in his wake.

Larry looked up from his racing forms as we approached. He ran a thick palm over his greasy hair and straightened his butterfly collar. His eyes groped my body in a way that left me craving a shower.

"Well, if it isn't Sabina Kane. How can I help you, sugar?" He completely ignored Slade.

"Is Zeke working tonight?"

Larry's eyes narrowed. "Sabina, you wound me. I was hoping you were coming to accept my offer to make a fang film.

I leaned back and tried to stifle my grimace.

Fang films were fetish videos geared toward the vamp population. The last time I saw Larry, he told me he could make me a star.

"Sorry, Larry, but I haven't changed my mind," I said. "I'm just looking for Zeke."

Larry's eyes narrowed. "You and everyone else."

"What do you mean?" Slade said, leaning in.

"Who the hell are you?" Larry demanded.

"This is my colleague Slade Corbin," I said.

Larry looked Slade over in what he probably thought was an intimidating stare. Slade simply stared back, cold as ice. I covered my smile with a hand. The thought of Larry intimidating anyone was laughable. The fact he was trying to intimidate a killing machine like Slade was downright hilarious.

Finally, under Slade's penetrating gaze, Larry cleared his throat. "Anyway, Zeke Corbin's dead to me. He was supposed to show up for work two days ago and I ain't heard one word."

"Any idea where we can find him?" I asked.

The male shrugged. "I think he hangs out at that strip club on Van Nuys."

"The Tit Crypt?"

He nodded. *Shit*, I thought. So far, all the clues were leading us around in circles.

"Do you have an address for him?" Slade asked.

Larry sighed. "Hold on, I got it here somewheres." His hefted his bulk from his stool and went to a file cabinet behind the counter. As he rifled through stacks of paper, he muttered to himself.

Slade and I exchanged a look. Chances were good Zeke wouldn't be at home, waiting for us to put a bullet between his eyes. But if we had the address, we could search the place for any clues on where he was hiding out.

Finally, Larry came back over and slapped a coffee-stained job application on the counter. "The address is on that," Larry said. "You find that asshole, you tell him he owes me two hundred dollars for all the videos he checked out and never returned."

I nodded and handed the paper to Slade. "Thanks, Larry. I owe you one."

Larry shifted on his seat and leaned in again. "Let me know if you change your mind about making a movie. I'd love to get you on my casting couch, if you know what I mean."

Out of the corner of my eye, I saw Slade's mouth twitch. "No, thanks," I said.

"Aw, c'mon. It'll be fun." He wiggled his bushy eyebrows suggestively.

"I said no." *Not just no*, I thought. *Hell, no.*

"Let me give you my card anyway." He pulled a greasy rectangle of paper from a stack at his elbow. "When you change your mind, call me. There's vamps out there'd pay good money to see a prime piece like you fangin' some pole."

Slade laughed out loud this time. I turned to

him with an eyebrow raised. The porn king wiggled his eyebrows again, pointing a bony finger at Slade. "Don't laugh, good-lookin'. I was talking to you."

One minute, Slade stood next to me with his mouth agape and his cheeks red. The next, the bell over the door rang and I got a nice view of Slade's ass before it disappeared.

∞

Back in the car, Slade's tight jaw hinted he was in no mood to be teased about Larry's parting shot. So, I bit my lip and avoided looking at him while I settled into my seat. He turned on the ignition before he finally spoke.

"I think we should hit Zeke's address tomorrow. I don't want to chance getting caught there near sunrise if shit goes down."

I glanced at the dashboard clock. It was about two hours until sunrise. Not a big deal for me, but getting caught at sunup would be an issue for my unwilling partner. The only benefit of being mixed-blood was my ability to be in the sun without suffering debilitating pain. Granted, it weakened me, but I didn't have to dive for shelter like every other vamp on the planet. "Makes sense."

"You hungry?"

"Liquid or solid?" I asked.

Slade smiled for the first time since I met him.

"Solid. I fed earlier."

"Now that you mention it, I could use a burger."

He put the car in gear. "I know just the place."

∞

Slade insisted we go to the window to order, instead of using the drive thru. Since I'd never been to In-N-Out Burger before, he insisted on ordering me something called a "Double-Double" with "large fries, well done." I wasn't sure exactly what any of that meant, but the heavenly aroma of grilled beef made my carnivore's heart go pitter-patter.

The chick in the orange apron handed over a box overflowing with burgers and cardboard boats filled with golden fries. Slade carried the feast to a small sitting area next to the parking lot.

He didn't wait for me to sit before digging into his food. I smiled at the utterly satisfied sounds escaping between his bites. For someone who'd come across so cold all night, Slade seemed to have a passion for food. He finally slowed down enough to notice I hadn't tried mine. He pointed at the box with his own burger. "Dig in," he said over a mouthful.

I wouldn't quite call the experience orgasmic, but it was a near thing. "Godsdamn!" I said after I'd inhaled half the thing.

"Right?" Slade said, shoving two fries into his

mouth.

We spent a few minutes munching companionably, watching cars pass by on Foothill Boulevard. Finally, I washed down my last bite with a gulp of cold soda. I was feeling good. Not just because of the burgers, either. What had started out as a disaster of a first mission—what with Slade being an ass—had turned into a pretty decent night.

"Slade?" I asked.

"Hmm?"

"Do you think we should review what we know so far?"

He grimaced, as if I'd just brought up a taboo subject. "Not much to review."

"But we have Zeke's personnel file. Maybe we should go through it for clues. You know, proof he's the one whose threatening the Dominae."

Slade raised an eyebrow. "Clues? Sabina, we're not detectives." He leaned in, whispering so the people at other tables wouldn't overhear. "We're assassins. It's not up to us to prove or deny Zeke's guilt. It's up to us to end him. Period."

"But the guy on the video was wearing a mask. How can we be sure it's this Zeke guy? After all, the perp could have opened the bank account under Zeke's name to throw us off his trail."

Slade cocked his head. "Slow down, Kojak. We're assassins, not detectives."

My face went hot at his dismissive tone. Ignoring him, I opened the file. Zeke's job application was on top. I scanned the page, looking for something. What, I had no idea. I scanned past the work history, since we already knew his last place of employment. Finally, my eyes landed on his chicken-scratched answers to a series of questions.

I snorted. "Listen to this. 'Why do you want to work at T&A Video?'" I looked up to make sure Slade was paying attention. He was taking a drink from his soda, but his eyes widened in a facsimile of real interest. "Zeke said, 'Cause I like to watch people fucking.'"

Slade spewed a mouthful of soda across the table. "At least he's honest," he said once he'd stopped choking.

I smiled and continued. "'Please discuss your previous experience in the adult film industry.' Zeke put 'Does whacking off to it three times a day count?'"

We both laughed so loud that the other customers started sending curious looks our way. Finally, I recovered enough to say, "The funniest part is that these answers got him the job."

Slade smiled and took another sip of his drink. A flash of fang peeked out when he pulled the straw away. "You surprised me tonight," he said, suddenly more serious.

"I know."

The corner of his mouth lifted. "I'm sorry if I was an asshole earlier. I just had a bad experience with the last rookie the Dominae saddled me with."

"Who was it?"

"Mischa Petrov."

I groaned and crumpled my burger wrapper, wishing it were Petrov's head.

"I take it you know her?"

"Unfortunately, yes." In addition to being my biggest competition in assassin school, Mischa Petrov was also my nemesis. She lorded my mixed blood over me whenever possible. And despite my higher grades, my grandmother had chosen Mischa as the *Primora* of the class. The honor ensured Mischa was fast-tracked into getting the plum jobs, unlike the rest of us, who had to serve time collecting tithes and tracking down petty criminals.

Slade laughed. "In addition to being completely incompetent, that female had the worst case of vagina dentata I've ever had the misfortune to experience."

I grimaced. "You fucked her?" My newfound respect for Slade took a nosedive.

He snorted and shook his head. "Are you kidding? I wouldn't let that she-devil anywhere near my unmentionables."

I smiled. "Good for you."

"Anyway," he said, "after that horrific experience, I didn't expect you'd be a pleasant surprise. Especially since—" He cut himself off and looked away quickly.

I nodded. "Let me guess: the mixed-blood

thing?" He nodded, looking sheepish. "Don't worry. I'm used to it."

He shifted uncomfortably on the small seat. "Anyway, I just wanted to apologize for earlier."

"Do you feel bad enough to split the take with me fifty-fifty?"

He threw back his head and laughed. "How about eighty-twenty?" His tone made it sound like he thought this offer was magnanimous.

I leaned forward, looking him in the eyes. "Sixty-forty."

He pursed his lips and narrowed his eyes at me. Finally, he sighed. "Seventy-thirty. Final offer."

"Gods, you're stubborn," I said.

He shrugged. "Despite your luck tonight, I'm still the lead on this mission. When we go in tomorrow, you're going to have to let me call the shots."

I saluted him. "Yes, sir."

His lips twitched. "Smartass."

∞

I let myself into my house and dropped my jacket and gun holster on the side table. After a night spent in the seediest establishment of the San Fernando Valley, it was time for a shower.

On my way past the kitchen, I ducked in to grab a beer from the fridge. I peeled back the tab on the can and chugged half of it before taking an extra for the trip to the bathroom.

The bathroom had pink tiles that I hated but not enough to make the effort of tearing them out.

I turned the water on to scalding and quickly stripped from my clothes. My shirt smelled like the inside of an ashtray mixed with grease and onions from the burger. I tossed it on the ground next to the rest of the week's discarded clothing.

The needles of water hit me between the shoulders. I gritted my fangs and relaxed into the welcome pain. Placing my palms against the tile, I lowered my head and let the heat and the pressure massage away the tension.

It's not that I considered the night's work a failure. Quite the opposite. We'd covered a lot of ground and found some useable clues about Zeke's whereabouts. But I was definitely feeling the pressure of needing to both prove to my grandmother that I could be trusted to work alone, and show Slade Corbin I had the stuff to become a great assassin like him.

I sighed and leaned my head back to wet it. While I lathered up, I thought about ways I could help the investigation move along. My fingers worked over my scalp, as if the massage would make my brain work faster. I rinsed my hair and took a long swig of the beer I'd brought in with me. Surely someone knew where to find Zeke Calebow.

I continued to ponder my options as I

completed my shower, dried off, and polished off the first beer. I pulled on a clean *Charlie's Angels'* T-shirt and some cut-off shorts before padding back into the living room.

My stereo sat on a shelf I'd created using cinder blocks and slats of wood. The records I played on it were stored in old milk crates. I flipped past the Clash, Joy Division, and Talking Heads. It was a Blondie night, so I grabbed the Parallel Lines album. Once that was on the turntable with the needle lowered, I retreated to the couch.

I found my black book sitting on the coffee table. Instead of being filled with names of eligible bachelors, it was filled with the names of pimps, bookies, loan sharks, and other types no one would want to take home to their mama—unless they wanted to get disowned.

With a sigh, I pondered who might be able to lead us to Zeke Calebow. I'd made it all the way to the Fs when a scratching noise echoed through the room. I cocked my head and looked toward the record player. Another scratch. No, definitely not coming from the hi-fi.

I rose and grabbed my gun from the side table. Keeping toes light on the hardwoods, I moved toward the door.

Scratch, scratch.

Keeping my gun in my right hand, I stood to the side of the door and reached for the knob with my left.

Scratchscratchscratch.

I pulled open the door. An orange streak flew through the air at my legs. Pain exploded on my bare skin.

"Ow, shit!"

The cat yowled, as if I was attacking it instead of the other way around. I kicked my leg out, but the godsdamned thing sank in its claws.

Grabbing it by the scruff of its neck, I ripped the cat off me. Stinging pain flared before the cold sensation of blood flow took over. But I was too busy holding the severely pissed-off feline away from my face.

"What the fuck is your problem?" I shook it a little.

"Yoooowl!"

I shook my head and stomped toward the open door. I didn't throw the cat, but I might have forgotten to gently lower it to the ground before I released it. The furball screamed its rage and pounced toward me. But I ran inside and slammed the door before it could get its claws in me again.

I leaned with my back against the door, my sides heaving from the adrenaline rush. Looking down, I inspected the angry red streaks on my shins. The wounds would heal quickly thanks to my vampire blood, but right then, I felt like I'd been shredded.

Scratch, scratch.

"Go away, Satan."

Scratchscratchyowlscratch.

Shaking my head, I hobbled over toward my beer. Being attacked by a cat with anger issues was thirsty business.

Blondie was now singing "Just Go Away," which was pretty fitting, all things considered. I shook my head and picked up the address book again.

Scraaaaatch!

"Damn it!" I tossed down the book and jumped off the couch.

This time, I left the gun on the table and walked directly to the door. But just in case, I picked up a baseball bat I kept near the door for emergencies. I cracked the door, careful to keep the bat between my legs and the opening.

An orange paw shot through the opening and swiped at the air. "Ha!" I taunted. "Not so tough now, are you?"

A hiss flew through the crack, followed by two more impotent swipes of the paw.

"What the hell is your problem, cat?" I opened the door a little wider. The hell beast looked up and dropped back on its butt.

The cat tilted its head and purred.

"What do you want?" Even as I asked the question, I realized how ridiculous it was to be having a conversation with an animal.

"Meow?"

Now that it had stopped trying to shred me into Sabina jerky, I realized how pitiful the thing looked. It was too thin, for one thing, and its fur was matted and dirty. It didn't have on a collar, so I didn't think it had a home. "Are you hungry?"

"Meow."

I pursed my lips and thought about my options. My fridge was full of beer, rotten milk, five bottles of mustard, and some fried rice from a few nights earlier. "Hold on." I shut the door, careful not to slam it on the cat's tail.

Almost immediately, the yowls and scratching started up again. "I said hold on!" I shouted over my shoulder. Throwing open my cupboards, I scanned the contents for something edible for a cat. "Aha!" I yelled in victory. Back behind a couple of boxes of pasta and a can of evaporated milk I don't remember buying, I found a single can of Spam.

I pulled back the top and sneered at the wet, hammy fragrance. It took a few good shakes to dump the lump of meat onto a paper plate. It looks about as appetizing as a brick of processed meat could, I guess. With a shrug, I carried the feast back to the door, which was rattling as the cat's scraping escalated.

Opening the door wide enough to fit the plate through, I dropped the feast in front of the panting feline. "Bon appétit."

The cat's face dove into the meat. Every few bites, its ears would fold back and it would emit a growl.

I crossed my arms and leaned against the

doorjamb. "Anyone ever tell you it's rude to hiss with your mouth full?"

Eventually, the beast settled into its meal. I knelt down and watched it. Closer, I could see the notch in its ear and the patches of missing fur that indicated I wasn't the only foe the cat had tried to best.

Something warm bloomed in my chest. I didn't recognize the feeling, but I figured it might be something close to affection. Maybe it was that I felt like I'd spent most of my life fighting, too. Maybe it was that, like my feline dinner guest, I was mostly alone in the world. And, maybe, just maybe, it was that I'd been forced to mold myself into a killer by my grandmother's order, when all I'd wanted to be was someone who comforted the lost.

I'd never forget the day Lavinia had told me that I wouldn't be allowed to enter the Temple to become an acolyte. She'd said that no mixed blood would ever be allowed into the sacred order. Besides, she'd said, she had other plans for me to be of service to the Dominae. A couple of weeks later, I arrived at the school where the Dominae's future Enforcers were trained.

I sighed and let my butt drop to the ground. The cat side-eyed me but didn't hiss this time. "Relax, Satan. I'm not going to hurt you."

The Spam was almost gone now. Satan looked up from the plate. Speckles of pink meat dotted its whiskers. A pink sandpaper tongue stuck out of its mouth to catch every last morsel. "You really were hungry."

"Meow."

I sighed and rose from my seat. As much as I'd like to sit in the predawn light with my new pal, I needed to finish strategizing for the next night with Slade. "All right, I need to go."

I scratched the fur between its ears but withdrew my hand quickly when its paw swiped at me again. This time instead of being pissed by the aggression, I was amused. "Take care of yourself, Satan."

The cat's head tilted and it watched me until I finally closed the door all the way. With a sigh, I walked back toward the sofa. This time, the drink I took from the beer was a contented one. With a smile, I leaned over the address book. Instead of going letter by letter, I fanned the pages and stopped on random pages.

I was on the letter H when a name leaped out at me. "Liliana Hartshorne," I said out loud, testing the sound of it. "Hmm."

I'd only met Lili once, and it hadn't been a pleasant experience. But if anyone knew where to find a horndog like Zeke Calebow, it was the faerie known as The *Faeriewood Madam*. "Gotcha," I breathed, feeling excited.

I would have called Slade to let him know I had a new lead, but the sun's pink rays were already creeping across the City of Angels. I'd tell him tomorrow when he came to pick me up. I took a celebratory drink, polishing off the beer.

Scratch, scratch!

Shaking my head, I rose off the couch. "What do you want now, Satan?" Emboldened by my earlier generosity, I opened the door all the way.

Satan sat on the threshold. I expected the beast to attack me again. Instead, it sashayed into my house like it belonged.

My mouth hanging open, I watched the orange ragamuffin stroll casually toward my sofa. It climbed onto pillow I'd knocked off earlier. Satan circled a few times counterclockwise and then two clockwise before laying itself on the pillow like a queen on a throne.

"By all means, make yourself at home." I considered shooing the uninvited guest back out the door, but I didn't have the heart. First of all, I'd kind of asked for it by offering the beast a smorgasbord of processed meatstuff. And second, now that its belly was full, Satan passed out on the pillow and was already snoring.

I sighed, accepting the inevitable. "All right," I said, "but just for tonight."

One eye opened and regarded me for a moment before closing again. And that was that.

∞

The next evening, my arms were loaded down as I pushed open the door. When I'd woken up that evening, I realized that if I was going to have a houseguest—even a temporary one—I'd need provisions. Satan had been hiding under the sofa and looked as if it didn't plan on coming out any time soon. So, I'd headed out to the closest pet store for some basics.

An hour later, I owned more cat toys, treats, and supplies than a crazy cat lady. The clerk at the store had talked me into a lot of extras, like flea dip (very necessary) and a skull-and-crossbones cat collar.

"Satan—I'm home." Balancing my burdens, I kicked the door shut with my heel and turned to face the living room.

"Holy shit!" The plastic cat crate dropped to the ground with a clatter. In its wake, the room felt ominously silent.

Satan sat in the middle of the room, watching me with unblinking eyes. The two-foot radius around its body looked normal. However, the rest of the room looked like the aftermath of the explosion of a shit bomb.

"Oh, gods!" Apparently, the Spam hadn't been my best idea.

In addition to the streaks of cat diarrhea all over every surface, including a few walls, Satan had taken his angst out on my sofa. The cushions were torn open and cotton batting and foam spilled out like entrails.

I let the remaining bags slide to the ground next to my feet. I only had half an hour before Slade was scheduled to pick me up. "I hate you so much right now," I said to the cat. It leaned back on its hip and slowly began licking at its nether region.

With a sigh, I went to the kitchen to look for rubber gloves, a bucket, cleaning solution, and paper towels. I grumbled to myself as I gathered the items and tried to decide whether I'd stuff and mount the cat after I killed it or if I'd simply leave its carcass on the porch to ward off any other demon cats who considered playing on my sympathies.

Twenty minutes later, I'd managed to clean up the worst of the mess. The process had involved some gagging and lots of cursing while Satan sat by and watched me. After I placed the garbage bags full of batting and paper towels out by the curb, I ran back inside for another shower.

I'd just managed to pull on my boots when the car horn honked at the curb. I came out of my bedroom to find Satan curled up in the remains of my sofa. "You and I are gonna have words when I get back," I said. The cat peeked open one eye, but didn't look at all worried.

I grabbed my keys, my gun, and my jacket on my way to the door. Opening the door, I stepped out onto the porch. But before I could shut it behind me, an orange furball streak past me. It jetted of the porch with a yowl that sounded suspiciously like a "fuck you" and disappeared into the woods surrounding my house. "Ungrateful asshole," I muttered.

Slade leaned against a black van at the curb. Judging from the frown on his face, he'd seen the cat's escape. "What the hell was that?"

"Unwelcome houseguest," I said.

He looked like he had other questions, but let them drop. "You ready?"

I climbed in and waiting for him to do the same before I asked about the molester-style van. "What happened to the Karmann Ghia?"

He shrugged. "This has better storage." He jerked his head toward the back. I looked over my shoulder and my eyes widened at the treasure trove of weaponry. He'd installed racks filled with guns, knives, crossbows, and various other implements of death. Along the opposite wall, a low bench featured manacles instead of seatbelts. Red shag carpet completed the dungeon-on-wheels look.

"Nice carpet," I said.

He turned the key and the engine roared to life. "Hides the blood."

∞

An hour later, we pulled up in front of Zeke's house in Glendale. Calling it a dump would have been generous. It looked like someone dropped a cinder block and then stuck a door and a couple windows on it. Although, the weeds, beer cans, and cigarette butts added a certain charm to the landscaping.

"Looks like peddling porn doesn't pay as much as I thought," Slade said.

"Yeah, extortion is much more lucrative," I replied, scanning the dark windows for signs of life. "Doesn't look like anyone's home."

"Let me grab some party favors, just in case," Slade said. He ducked back into the cargo area. He opened his leather blazer and started filling interior pockets with assorted stabby things.

Let me just say, nothing is sexier than watching a male strap on weapons. Slade was no exception. For an ass, he had a certain alpha-male sexiness going for him. But I knew better than to entertain those thoughts for very long. I needed to keep my mind on the mission. So, I took my eyes off his physique and focused on his weapons. That's when I noticed he didn't bother grabbing any guns.

"No firearms?" I asked, checking the chamber of my own.

He paused. "Never use 'em." He pulled up the leg of his bell-bottoms and strapped a nylon sheath around his ankle. Into that went three wooden spikes.

"Why not?"

He paused, as if considering the matter for the first time. Finally, he shrugged. "Just don't like guns."

"Oh, I get it," I said. "You're old."

He laughed. "I'm only sixty, Sabina. Hardly old by vampire standards."

"You're joking. Sixty?"

He shook his head and grabbed a few throwing stars made of applewood from the shelf. Judging by the smirk on his face, I'd managed to amuse him. As much as I didn't like being the source of anyone's amusement, I had to look at him with grudging respect. To have accomplished so much as an assassin at such a young age was mind-blowing.

"Ready?" he said, breaking into my thoughts. I nodded and cocked my gun. I might want to learn from Slade, but I drew the line at giving up my weapon.

∞

We went in through the back door. In his haste to leave, Zeke must have forgotten to lock it. I shook my head at the oversight. For someone who'd managed to elude us this long, Zeke sure was an idiot.

The kitchen stunk like rotting trash and spoiled food. Even in the dark, I could see the dishes piled up in the sink and the mountain of pizza boxes stacked next to the overflowing trash can. Spatters of food crusted the harvest yellow fridge and the avocado green counters.

Two doors led off the kitchen to other rooms in the house. Slade pointed to the right, indicating we should split up. I nodded and went through the breakfast area.

The only signs of life from my perspective were cockroaches crawling over forgotten cereal bowls and glasses coated with dried blood. Zeke, in addition to being a pain in my ass, also appeared to be the biggest slob I'd ever encountered.

I moved silently to the corner leading into the living room. When no sounds came from the room beyond, I slowly turned the corner with my gun ready to shoot anything that moved. Maybe I was being paranoid, but carelessness didn't pay the bills. More than one enforcer had gotten dead by being cocky.

This room was decorated in bachelor chic. Posters of a scantily clad Farrah Fawcett-Majors and the Dallas Cowboy cheerleaders lined the walls. The furnishings consisted of a battered orange Barcalounger parked in front of a TV the size of a Volkswagen. I moved through the room quickly and headed toward the back hallway, which I assumed led to the bedrooms.

Through the doorway, I encountered a linen closet filled with *Hustler* magazines and ratty towels. A sound to my left had me swinging my gun around. Slade held up his hands and stopped. I blew out a breath and lowered the gun a fraction.

"Anything?" I whispered.

He shook his head. "All clear. You check that last room?"

A closed door waited on our right, which

presumably led to a guest room or office. I shook my head and moved toward it. Slade had my back. Not that it made me feel any better. Despite his obvious experience in the field, his presence unsettled me. I was used to working alone, and adding a partner to the mix brought in all sorts of variables I couldn't control.

Still, I sucked in some air and turned the knob. When no one rushed me or shot me in the face, I let out my breath and walked in. Slade clicked on a flashlight behind me and shined it into the stuffy room. Dust particles glittered in the beam while my eyes adjusted. Once they focused again, I made out a utilitarian metal desk pushed up against the far wall. Confident we were alone in the house, I walked over and clicked on the desk lamp.

I busied myself opening desk drawers, rooting around for any clue of Zeke's whereabouts. All I got for my effort were a few back issues of *Playboy*, gummy rubber bands, and a matchbook.

"Um, Sabina?"

I pocketed the matchbook, and looked over my shoulder to see what had Slade sounding spooked. He had his back to me, his gaze intent on the wall.

At first, I thought more beer posters plastered the wall. But when I turned around to get a better look, my mouth dropped open. The same collage used as a backdrop in the video covered the wall.

Zeke had crafted his very own serial killer-esque *objet d'art* out of newspaper clippings, photographs, bits of string, and what appeared to be bloody handprints. "Godsdamn, that's creepy."

I moved closer, careful not to touch anything. Zeke had been a busy boy. Upon closer inspection, I realized the pictures and clippings all served to prove the existence of vampires. From shots of vamps sucking on the necks of victims to headlines about unexplained murders, he had enough evidence to convince even those most doubtful mortal that the stuff of their nightmares not only existed but walked down the same streets and ate at the same restaurants as the Sons of Adam.

"He wasn't bluffing," Slade said quietly. "He really intends to expose us to the mortals."

I backed away from the scent of dried blood and newsprint ink. "Do you have a camera in that van of yours?"

Slade opened his mouth to answer but stilled when a loud crash echoed through the apartment. The sound came from the other end of the house, probably the kitchen. I grabbed my gun and went to turn off the light. The room fell into darkness. Something about darkness always amplifies sounds. And this was no different. My breath sounded harsh to my ears as I listened to footsteps advancing through the house.

I glanced at Slade. He held a finger to his lips and went to stand with his back against the wall next to the door. I took point in the corner, diagonal to the doorway, ready to shoot first and ask questions later.

Floorboards creaked in the living room. Amateur, I thought. Or someone who wasn't expecting two vampires to be waiting for them. I crouched down in the shadows, giving myself the advantage of being able to see the intruder before they saw me.

The darkness in the hall shifted. I aimed the gun directly at the silhouette, tracking the figure. Finally, the shadow crossed the threshold and stopped.

"Stop right there." Slade's calm voice sounded unnaturally loud in the dark.

The intruder panicked, squeezing the trigger of the gun in his hand. Three more panic shots followed in quick succession. I covered my head with my hands as a shot zinged past my ear. "Godsdammit!"

"Stop!" Slade yelled. A scuffle sounded from the doorway. A female gasp followed by a male grunt.

I dove for the lamp on the desk. Light spilled through the room just in time for me to catch Mischa Petrov kneeing Slade between the legs. Gods love him, he held his ground, knocking the gun from her hand.

"Mischa, stop!" I yelled.

But she wasn't done fighting. The idiot was so pumped up on adrenaline, she wasn't thinking.

"You scared the shit out of me!" she yelled at Slade, swiping at him and hissing like a feral cat. She was even dressed like Catwoman in her one-piece black jumpsuit, which left little to the imagination.

I grabbed her arms and tore her away from Slade. She panted like an injured animal, ready to strike again. Blood covered Slade's lower lip, and two deep scratch marks bled freely next to his eye. Seeing the needless injuries, something snapped. I could understand why she shot without looking, but her disgraceful display of fear after the fact disgusted me.

"What the fuck were you thinking? You could have killed us!" I yelled. She jerked away and rounded on me.

"Me?" she spat. "You two were skulking in the shadows like a couple of thieves."

"I told you to stop." Slade said it in the same tone one might use to share the time. His complete lack of anger impressed me. Sure, he was probably pissed on the inside. But outside? Total control. That was the sign of a real professional. Unlike some bitches I could mention.

Mischa seemed to have collected some of her composure. She smoothed her palms over her ruby-red Crystal Gayle hair, which, in my opinion, was completely ridiculous for an assassin. Now that she's gotten control of herself, she transformed back into her typical dragon lady persona. "Sorry, Slade. If I'd known it was you, I never would have fired." She smiled at him in a way that reminded me of a lion eyeing a particularly plump gazelle.

"Your lack of control makes you a danger to both yourself and anyone working with you."

Her eyes narrowed. "Fuck you, Slade."

"I'd rather gnaw off my own arm, thanks."

I didn't bother to cover my grin. "Looks like you've lost one of your admirers, Mischa."

She turned on me, practically spitting venom. "Shut up, mixed-blood. No one asked for your opinion."

I clenched my teeth and glared at her, refusing to let her get the best of my temper. I turned to Slade. "Can we go now?"

Slade shook his head. "Not until Mischa explains what she's doing here."

Mischa crossed her arms. "I'm looking for Zeke."

Slade's eyes narrowed. "This is my hit, Mischa. Back the fuck off."

"What are you talking about? The Dominae assigned me to this case."

"Bullshit."

She smiled, showing a flash of fang. "Guess they figured you'd be handicapped with the half-breed." She sent a venomous glance my way. "Face it, Slade. With her slowing you down, it'll be a miracle if you win this one."

∞

I was still stewing when Slade started the van. After Mischa's insults, he had to physically remove me from Zeke's house. Lucky for her he had, because I'd been about two seconds from going Three Mile Island on her ass.

If Slade felt angry about the fact the Dominae brought Mischa in as insurance, he wasn't showing it.

"Stop sulking," Slade said. "If you let her get a rise out you, she'll win every time."

"I'm not sulking," I lied. "I was strategizing."

"Mmm-hmm," he said. "Do you always pout when you strategize?"

That was it. Between Satan's dramatic departure and Mischa's poisonous words, I'd been insulted enough for one night. I turned to Slade with a glare. "You know what? I don't think this partnership's going to work out for me after all."

He didn't seem impressed by my declaration. "Oh, I see." He nodded, as if he'd just had a revelation. "You're giving up."

"No, I'm not. I just prefer to work alone."

Slade sighed. "That's not an option and you know it. Until I give the Dominae the all clear on you, you're not allowed to pursue perps on your own."

I rammed my fist into the dashboard. He was right, but I didn't like it. I'd worked my ass off in assassin school and paid my dues for close to a decade to get this chance. Having to shadow an arrogant ass was insult added to injury.

"You're going to pay for that," Slade said calmly, looking at the dent I'd left in the dashboard.

"Fuck off." Anger and shame warred for supremacy in my gut. Anger because I was sick and tired of being underestimated. Shame because I was having a tantrum in front of an assassin of Slade's caliber.

"Sabina?" he said quietly.

I whipped toward him. "What?"

"Where should we go next?"

I stopped cold. "What?"

"Which word didn't you understand?" he said, brow furrowing.

I blew out a breath, feeling like an ass for my display of temper. "No. What I meant was, are you sure you still want to work with me?"

He frowned. "Why wouldn't I?"

I crossed my arms, hating him a little bit for making me spell it out. "Well, for one, not many vampires would choose a mixed-blood for a partner. And the Dominae obviously think I'm a fuckup, so I can't imagine why you'd bother."

He laughed at me. I narrowed my eyes, not understanding how anything I'd said was funny. "Grow up, little girl. This isn't about you and your pride. It's about the job." He paused and looked me in the eye. "You want to be a good assassin?"

I assumed the question was rhetorical, so I didn't answer at first. But he remained silent for so long, it became apparent he expected an answer. I lifted my chin. "I don't want to be good. I want to be the best."

He bobbed his head, obviously approving of the answer. "You'll never be the best if you allow your feelings to get in the way of the job. So, suck it up, sweetheart. Kill Zeke, collect the reward, and move on. Self-pity has no place in our line of work."

On the outside, I probably looked at stubborn as ever. My arms stayed crossed, my chin stayed raised, and my eyes stayed narrowed. But on the inside, his words washed through me like ice water. It wasn't easy to accept that my emotions had been getting the best of me. But he was right. The longer I let my grandmother's underestimation of my abilities hurt me, the longer it would take for me to earn her respect. Females like Lavinia Kane didn't respect whiners. They respected doers—like Slade.

"Besides," Slade continued. "Do you really want to let Mischa win?"

At that moment, something shifted inside me. Fighting against the prejudices I faced was a waste of time. From now on, I'd focus on being the best assassin I could be. I'd start by working with Slade and learning everything I could from him. And lesson number one was most definitely learned.

"Our next stop is an estate called Faerywood. It's in Hollywood Hills off Mulholland Drive."

The corner of Slade's mouth lifted, and he nodded approvingly. "Yes, ma'am."

∞

A massive Tudor-style mansion stood beyond the massive iron gates in front of the van's headlights. Slade clicked the intercom.

"Yes?" The male's voice had a snooty British accent.

"We're here to see Liliana Hartshorne," he said.

"Do you have an appointment?"

"No, but—"

"I'm sorry, sir, but access to Faerywood is by appointment only."

I leaned across Slade to speak into the speaker. "Tell her it's Sabina Kane. We're here on Dominae business."

A pregnant pause followed my statement. Instead of a verbal response, the gates swept open.

Slade flashed me a grin. "Sometimes, working for the Dominae has its advantages."

I chuckled. "The first time I met Liliana Hartshorne, she was at the Dominae's mansion, begging for Lavinia not to kill one of her favorite girls."

He raised a brow for an explanation.

"One of the Dominae's guards had fallen in love with the faery whore. Lavinia had the vamp put down and was demanding the girl be sacrificed as well, to send a message to the races to remember the Blood Covenant."

The sacred document I mentioned was an agreement signed by all the Dark Races way back to keep peace among the races. Apparently, it was okay for vampires to pay faeries for sex, but it was not okay for them to fall in love.

"What happened to the girl?" Slade pulled the van around the circular drive.

"Dead," I said. "But Lavinia made it up to Liliana by gifting her this estate."

His lips twitched. "Guess that explains the easy access."

He put the van in park and turned off the ignition. "So, what's the plan?"

On our way, I'd filled him in on a Hartshorne's role as a madam. As the head of the most successful Dark Races brothel in Los Angeles, it was her job to know who was fucking whom and for how much. I figured if anyone might be able to connect us to someone who knew Zeke's whereabouts, it was the faerie madam.

"Straightforward," I said. "Liliana can smell bullshit from a mile away. No sense trying to trick information out of her."

He nodded and opened his door. I met him at

44

the front steps. The massive, arched wooden door was surrounded by a portico covered in a blooming moonflower vine. Slade pressed the button, and a few moments later, a short man in a tuxedo opened the door.

"Miss Kane." He bowed formally. "Madam Hartshorne will receive you and your guest in the drawing room."

I nodded and stepped over the threshold into a massive, two-story foyer. A winding staircase was across from the doorway and led up to a balcony with wrought-iron railings. The butler, who had delicately pointed ears peeking from under his black hair, led us to a room on the right.

This space was obviously where the girls who worked in the house received their guests. From what I'd heard, the procedure was for the males to sit in one of the comfortable leather chairs with a brandy or pint of blood while they looked over a lineup of fae "escorts." Each of Hartshorne's girls had a specialty so as to accommodate any customer's more adventurous tastes.

"She'll be with you shortly," the butler said in his refined accent. "Please have a seat."

Slade and I exchanged a humorous look at all the formality. Considering there was probably a ton of kinky sex going on upstairs, it was hard to reconcile the elegant surroundings of the main floor.

"This place is no joke," Slade observed. He settled into one of the wingback chairs beside the fireplace. "I feel like I should be wearing a smoking jacket in this thing."

I smirked, but before I could respond, a swirl of red appeared in the doorway. Liliana Hartshorne wore layers of cherry-red chiffon and an emerald-green silk turban with a sparkly brooch in the center. She had large green eyes like a china doll's with heavily lids and thick lashes. The audacity of her getup was probably chosen to compensate for her diminutive stature. Like most female faeries, she was well below five feet tall, and the kitten heels on her feet probably added three inches.

"Sabina." Her voice was husky, as if she swilled whiskey and smoked cigars to achieve the affect. "Please introduce me to your friend."

Slade rose from his seat and moved forward. "Slade Corbin, ma'am," he said, doing my job for me. "A pleasure."

Her eyes sparkled. "Not yet, but it might be if you play your cards right." She extended her fingers, which were studded with jewels, to the vampire for a kiss.

The corner of Slade's mouth tilted up, but he bent over dutifully and placed a kiss on her knuckles. "Thank you for receiving us," he said, smooth as silk. "We know your time is valuable."

I suppressed the shock that followed watching him work the madam so smoothly. But I supposed one didn't spend so long being an assassin without picking up some skills at manipulation. Either way, the madam ate it up like a cat lapping cream.

"Impudent boy," she said. "Wherever has Lavinia been hiding you?"

He released her hand and stepped back a respectable distance. "No place respectable, that's for sure."

She threw back her head and brayed like an ass. I barely managed not to roll my eyes.

"We're here on a matter of some urgency," I prompted.

She flicked a glance my way, as if she'd forgotten my presence. "Everything with the Dominae is urgent. Why don't we have a drink first?"

Slade opened his mouth, but since he appeared to be about to accept her offer, I interrupted. "Perhaps another time," I said. "We really are in a hurry."

The madam sniffed. "Suit yourself." She turned a cold shoulder and went to the bar to help herself to a drink. Slade shot me an annoyed glance, but I ignored it.

"Have you ever had a customer named Zeke Calebow?"

She paused in the process of pouring a clear liquid into a tumbler and looked up. "Doesn't sound familiar, but I can't be sure. I meet so many people in my line of work."

I didn't believe that for an instant. A businesswoman like Liliana made her business to know everything about her customers.

"Perhaps you could check your records?" Slade asked.

She smiled at him. "I'm afraid my personal secretary is otherwise engaged at the moment." She looked up toward the ceiling, as if to indicate the secretary was taking a special kind of dictation. "Do you perhaps have a picture of Mr. Calebow? I never forget a face."

Slade held up the picture of Zeke that Tanith gave us. She sauntered over with her drink and took the photo from him. Looking down at it, she paused and looked up with a frown. "This is Jacques Dubois."

I tilted my head. "No," I said slowly. "That's Zeke Calebow."

"But that's impossible. Not three nights ago, this man came to this very spot and introduced himself as Monsieur Dubois. He had a passport and everything."

I exchanged a confused look with Slade. "The man in that picture isn't French; he's American, and he's trying to extort a large sum of cash from the Dominae."

The faery blanched. "Impossible."

"I assure you it's very much possible. My guess is he secured the fake passport in preparation for fleeing the country."

"Goddess help us," she said. "This is

horrible." Gone were the affectations she'd displayed like peacock feathers earlier. In their place was a hand-wringing female. "Hold on." She minced over to a harvest yellow rotary phone on the wall. It took a good thirty seconds to compose the number using the rotary dial.

"You want to fill us in on what's got you so upset?" I asked.

She held up an impatient finger, which was topped with a long red fingernail. Then she ignored us completely as she spoke rapidly into the phone. I leaned forward to catch the words, but she quickly hung up the receiver.

She sighed loudly and turned back toward us. "The head of my security team is on his way down."

"Why?" Slade asked.

"Because three nights ago, the man you're looking for strolled into this establishment, pretending to be a French aristocrat, and rented by best girl for the entire week."

My mouth fell open. "Wait, you let him walk out of here with a female?" The idea of the freckle-faced vampire in the picture affecting a convincing French accent was ludicrous, which meant Liliana was more convinced by the promise of money than any sort of good sense.

She nodded with an expression on the border between panic and rage. "And that's not even the worst part."

"I can't imagine what would be worse than

that," Slade said in an arid tone.

Liliana crossed her arms. "I believed him when he said he was from a wealthy French vampire lineage, so I let him walk out without paying!"

I shook my head. "You're joking. What kind of madam are you to let a complete stranger walk out of here with one of the females you're supposed to protect?"

The madam's back went up. "He had letters vouching for him!"

Slade's eyebrows shot up. "Which are easier to forge than a passport."

She opened her mouth to respond, and from the looks of things the shine, she'd taken to my partner had definitely dulled, but before the words left her mouth, a male arrived. Judging from his height and the copious amounts of body hair, he was a werewolf.

"Rolf, thank goodness," Liliana said. "We have a bit of a situation."

The were came forward. He wore a brown business suit with a cream colored shirt that had a butterfly collar. His shaggy hair made him look like one of the Bee Gees—the manly one with the beard. "Who are they?" He nodded toward Slade and me.

Liliana quickly performed introductions and filled her head of security in on the situation. As she spoke, his expression went from curious to downright predatory. "I knew there was something off about that piece of shit," he growled.

"There's really no sense in beating yourselves up about the mistake," Slade said in a calm tone. "The important thing now is to figure out where he took her."

Gods, he was smooth. He acted like we were doing them a favor, but we needed them more than they needed us.

Rolf crossed his arms. In his right hand was a file folder. "Why would we give you any information? This is our business now."

I mirrored his stance. "Because I'm fairly certain neither of you want the girl you sent off with him killed."

Liliana's expression became stricken. "You wouldn't dare."

I shrugged. "It's not up to us, really. You know how Lavinia is."

The madam's face hardened as she looked at me. But to Rolf, she said, "Give them the address."

The werewolf didn't look happy, but he followed orders regardless. He opened the folder and removed a handwritten receipt. At the top was the name Jacques Dubois, along with an address in Long Beach. I scanned lower to see the services listed as a week of escorting by a faery named Pansy Foxglove. The amount listed as the amount due was more than I paid for rent on my house in a year. Underneath the amount due, a messy scrawl spelled out the name Jacques

Dubois. It had the insecure slant of a man unused to signing the name.

I looked up. "You really let him walk out of here owing this much?" My question was mostly rhetorical.

Liliana's chin came up. "He left collateral."

I raised a brow. "Oh, yeah?"

She nodded. "An heirloom brooch he said belonged to his grandmother, the Duchess of Foie Gras." Two red spots appeared on her overly made-up cheeks, as if saying it out loud brought home the extent of her errors in judgment.

"If I were you, I wouldn't go pawning that brooch anytime soon," Slade said.

"What assurances do we have that you will not kill Pansy?" The madam's demeanor shifted from embarrassed to determined. Despite the ridiculous decisions she'd made, it was clear she actually cared a lot about her girls.

Slade pursed his lips and thought it over for a moment. "You agree to give us twenty-four hours to make our move on Calebow, and we'll ensure your girl gets home safe and sound."

Rolf turned to look at his boss, his expression clearly indicating he was not in favor of this plan. I didn't know a lot about werewolves, but it didn't take a genius to know the breed had fierce hunting instincts. The prospect of hunting down a shitbag like Zeke Calebow had to have his predatory instincts thrumming.

But Liliana Hartshorne was no fool—despite her weakness for promissory notes from fake European royalty. "It's a deal," she said. "I'll expect updates."

Slade nodded and stepped forward. The madam held out her ringed hand to shake on it. But my smooth-operator partner grabbed the tips of her fingers and looked her in the eye as he kissed the knuckles again. The move elicited a growl from Rolf and an eye-roll from me.

The madam, however, was charmed. "After you bring Pansy home, I'd be happy to offer you the works—free of charge."

Slade's smile didn't waver, but his Adam's apple bobbed as if fighting a dry heave. "You're far too kind."

The madam pulled her bright eyes and seductress's smile from my partner to look at me. "You too, of course," she said in a grudging tone.

I frowned. "Thanks, but I'm not into faeries or females."

She tilted her head. "Hmm. I thought maybe you followed in your grandmother's footsteps."

My mouth fell open.

The faery smiled. "Lavinia loves her some faery pussy."

All the blood drained from my face, leaving nothing but coldness and nausea behind. Before I could comment—or vomit—Slade grabbed my arm and led me out of the room, trailing behind us promises to be in touch.

When we made it outside, I bent over next to the van with my hands on my knees. I sucked in a few lungfuls of the cool night air, hoping it would scour the images Liliana's parting shot had planted in my brain. From my bent-over position, I saw Slade's boots appear to my right.

"If you're going to vomit, do it before you get in the van."

"I'm fine." I pressed my lips together and pushed myself back into a standing position. He cocked an eyebrow at me. "Do you think she was telling the truth?"

"About Lavinia?"

I nodded.

He shrugged. "Who cares?"

I stepped forward. "You're joking, right? Lavinia Kane is the ultimate enforcer of the Black Covenant. If it got out that she had sex with faeries, it would be devastating for the Dominae."

Slade crossed his arms and shot me a level look. "Sabina, are you really going to believe the catty comment of a woman who believed that a schmuck like Zeke Calebow was fucking French aristocracy?"

I tilted my head and thought it over. "Guess you're right."

"Of course I am." He put a hand on my shoulder. "Most likely she was just trying to start some shit because she's still pissed at Lavinia for killing that girl you told me about when we got here."

"Good point." I nodded and sighed. I glanced at my watch. "You want to head to this address they gave us now?"

Slade glanced at his watch. "It's getting early. The address is in Long Beach, which is like forty-five minutes away at least. Let's call it a night and I'll see if I can figure out whether the address is a residence or a business."

I nodded. "I'd feel a lot better going in prepared than showing up to ambush so close to sunrise, too."

"It's settled then," he said. "Tomorrow night, we terminate the bastard."

∞

When I got into the van the next night, Slade tossed a page from the phonebook into my lap.

"What's this?" I held the page up to the light. An advertisement for a hotel called Jack's Hideaway was circled in red pen.

"I tracked down the address last night. From what I can tell, it's a no-tell motel not far from the Queen Mary."

"Did you call?"

"I called. Looks like Mr. Jacques Dubois checked in four nights ago."

"What an idiot," I said. "Let's go."

We hit the 710 about six o'clock. Big mistake. Traffic didn't just crawl; it oozed. I settled into my seat, prepared for a long wait.

"Thanks for the pep talk last night," I said.

Slade looked at me out of the corner of his eye. "No problem. We all need a good kick in the ass every now and then."

"I find it hard to imagine that you ever need one."

He laughed. "You'd be surprised. I won't lie to you; the life of an assassin isn't easy. Since you're just starting out, it's best to learn that early."

My life hadn't ever been what anyone would consider easy, I thought. "How long have you been doing this?"

He shrugged. "About thirty years now."

"Do you ever regret it? Becoming an assassin, I mean."

He paused, as if weighing his response. "Sometimes. It's a lonely life. And I have to admit I don't always see eye to eye with the Dominae." His words came out in a measured tone, each carefully chosen.

"I can see that, I guess. Have you ever killed someone and regretted it?"

He shifted in the seat. "Traffic's heavy tonight."

And with that, the door slammed shut on our conversation. The shades were drawn. And the "do not disturb" sign flashed like neon in the dark car.

∞

Jack's Hideaway squatted on the side of the freeway like a beggar. The sign featured flashing neon palm trees and advertised rooms by the hour.

"Charming place," I observed as Slade pulled into the parking lot. The peeling turquoise doors opened directly onto the parking lot. The cars of choice for the discerning Hideaway patron seemed to be semi trailers and jalopies.

After making a circle of the building to make sure Zeke couldn't slip through a rear exit, Slade pulled into a parking space at the far end of the lot.

"Okay, his room's on the second floor," Slade pointed to the door next to the metal stairwell.

"You think he's in there?"

Slade nodded. "My gut tells me yes. But I'm worried about the faery locked in there with him. Be prepared for anything." He went into the back of the van and started filling his pockets with weapons. "I'll take point. You hang back. If he gets past me, put a bullet between his eyes. Got it?"

I nodded. My heart kicked up a notch. It was finally happening. My first kill.

The parking lot was deserted. Beyond the hush of traffic from the freeway, our movements up the stairs were muted. It wouldn't cover the sound of gunfire, though, so I'd made sure to slip on a silencer.

Slade took point on the left side of the door and I took the right, ready to get his back. Staying to the side, Slade knocked on the door.

"What?" a surly male voice called from inside. Zeke.

"Maintenance."

"Fuck off." The voice was closer now. A shadow passed over the peephole. Slade didn't bother responding. He kicked the door in, slamming it into Zeke's face. The pudgy vamp fell back with his hands over his nose, screaming blood murder.

With the vampire not blocking the door, I could finally see into the room. The bedspread and sheets had been kicked off to the floor. An overturned lamp lay drunkenly on the side table. A painting that presumably had once hung over the headboard was piled in the corner. The canvas was ripped and its frame splintered. I took all that in quickly, along with the lack of female.

"Where's Pansy Foxglove?" I demanded.

Zeke lay on the ground. His nose bled freely but his eyes burned with anger. "Who the fuck are you?"

Slade stepped over the threshold into the room. "We're your worst nightmare, asshole. Did you really think the Dominae wouldn't track you down?"

The vampire's rapidly swelling eyes widened. In the next heartbeat, he leapt off the ground and barreled past Slade. I braced myself, but the vampire's momentum knocked me off my feet. I fell on my ass just as he launched over the railing and took off across the parking lot.

"Fuck!" Slade yelled and took off after him. "Find the girl!" he shouted over his shoulder.

I scrambled to my feet with a few choice curses of my own. Looking for the girl would mean I might miss the big finale, but I also knew if that girl died, we'd have the faery madam's werewolf goon on our asses.

I ran into the room. "Pansy?" I called. A weak noise came from the direction of the bathroom. Like a lot of hotel rooms, the sink sat in a counter outside the bathroom proper. The rusty taps leaked brown water into the basin. I looked toward the door, which was closed, but no light came from underneath.

"Pansy?" I whispered, not wanting to scare the girl.

Another whimper, this time louder. I reached for the door handle and carefully pushed the panel. The door hit something solid and a responding screech sounded.

"Shit, sorry." I peeked through the opening and froze.

A mass of wet hair and tears mixed with blood had been bound to the base of the toilet. She was gagged and naked.

"Great Mother protect us," I breathed. Despite my disgust over the obvious abuse the girl had suffered, I marshaled my limbs into action. "I'll be right back," I promised the girl.

I ran back into the other room and grabbed the comforter. This wasn't the kind of hotel that offered fluffy white robes to its guests, so the bedspread would have to do until I could locate her clothes.

Back in the bathroom, I carefully covered her with the spread. Her eyes were wide and haunted, and she shied away from the contact. "Shh," I said. "I'm here to help you. My name is Sabina."

She looked unsure but finally nodded. I reached up and pulled down the gag. She worked her jaw experimentally and earned a wince for the effort. She swallowed hard, as if to rewet a dry throat. "Jacques?" she croaked.

"My partner is handling him."

She nodded and let out a shuddering breath. I waited a moment to make sure she wasn't about to lose her shit, but she stayed quiet. With a decisive nod, I took a look at mass of knots in the rope Zeke had used to tie her to the commode. Removing a knife from my boot, I raised it to cut through the rope.

"My boss doesn't know where I am," Pansy whispered. "She'll be so angry with me."

The last knot gave, releasing her hands. She raised them and began to rub against the rope burns on her wrists. I shook my head. "Liliana helped us find you. I promise she won't be angry with you."

I knelt down and helped her stand. "Are you hurt anywhere critical?"

She shook her head. "I don't think so. He knocked me around some." This statement was unnecessary. She had cuts on her jaw and cheekbones, but it had been the burns I'd noticed on her breasts and thighs that had me worried. As if she'd read my thoughts, she said, "He used a cigarette." A shudder rushed through her small body. I pulled her closer and helped her through the door.

We were limping toward the bed when the door burst open again. Only, instead of Slade returning to say he'd killed Zeke, it was Liliana's werewolf, Rolf.

The girl cried out at the noise and her whole body shuddered, as if she'd been worried it was Zeke coming back for more. I looked down and realized she'd squeezed her eyes shut. "Pansy," I said softly, "it's okay. It's just Rolf."

Her eyes opened and she sagged against me. I helped her to the bed and lowered her to the edge. When I looked up again, Rolf was frozen in the doorway. If the rage on his face was anything to go by, he was having some problems processing what he was seeing.

I crossed my arms. "You said we had twenty-four hours."

He dragged his gaze from the faery huddled on the bed to glare at me. "So sue me." Dismissing me, he rushed across the room to kneel before

Pansy. With a surprisingly gentle touch, he took the small hand lying on her lap. He looked down at the angry red wounds from the rope. "Pansy?" he whispered.

As if his gentleness was the final straw, she let out a wail and fell into the werewolf's arms. He wrapped his arms around her and cradled her small body in his lap. Something told me their relationship went beyond simple protector and prostitute. I looked away from the intimacy of the scene. "I'm going to go help Slade," I said. But neither of them looked up. Knowing the girl was now in good hands, I spun on my heel and ran out the door.

On the balcony, I stopped to listen. My vampire hearing meant I could hear more than a mortal. I closed my eyes and blocked out the sounds of traffic from the freeway and the TVs coming out of the other rooms. Sure enough, the sound of fists against flesh reached me.

I jumped over the railing and shot across the parking lot.

Somewhere behind me, I heard a door slam, followed by the sound of high heels on pavement. A familiar female voice cursed loudly. I didn't look back, but I'd have bet cash money Mischa followed us to the hotel, hoping to cut in on the action.

I pumped my legs faster and turned down the alley between the hotel and the liquor store beside it. I came out the other end of the alley in time to see Slade and Zeke duking it out beside a Dumpster.

I paused. Why the hell was Slade bothering tussling with the vampire? He should have already killed the bastard. But even as I thought that, relief washed through me. I hadn't missed out on the kill, and judging from what I'd just left behind in the room, I definitely wanted to be part of the main event.

Up ahead, Zeke clasped his fists together and slammed them into the side of Slade's head. The assassin stumbled. Not far, but just enough for Zeke to jump on top of the Dumpster. Then he leaped up to grab the bottom of a fire escape ladder. Pulling it down, he scrambled up the ladder onto the platform. Then he pulled the ladder up behind him. From there, he climbed up a series of footholds to the building's roof.

"Slade?" I called.

Slade shook his head as if Zeke's strike had rung his bell pretty good. "Go around the front of the building in case he comes back down!"

I stopped, panting for breath. "Why me?"

"Really? You're going to argue now?" He looked over his shoulder at Mischa, who was running toward us in her five-inch heels.

"Fine, but if you reach him first, wait until I catch up."

Slade nodded impatiently and jumped up on the Dumpster. "Go!"

I backtracked, zooming past Mischa in the

alley without a second glance. I heard her skitter to a halt. "Where are you going?" She turned to follow me.

I ignored her and ran around to the front of the motel. A black Trans Am with a snarling wolf on the hood was peeling out of the parking lot. Guess that meant Rolf had decided to get Pansy out of there rather than wait for us. Fine by me. The girl needed medical attention, and the less bodies around, the better.

The lobby was deserted, thank the gods. My boots clomped across the linoleum toward the stairs. The door opened behind me and Mischa's heels joined my boots in echoing off the walls.

"Sabina," she whisper-yelled. "What's going on?"

I needed to ditch her before she got in the way. Skidding to a halt, I turned. "Mischa, thank the goddess you're here. Zeke's on his way out the front door," I lied. "You stay here and bag him when he comes your way."

She narrowed her eyes, trying to figure out if she could trust me. "Where are you going?"

I heaved a big sigh. "You don't want to help, fine. But you can explain to the Dominae why you let him go after he escapes again."

She lifted her chin. "All right, but if I bag him, I'm not splitting the money with you."

"Whatever. Just stay there and make sure he doesn't get away."

Without waiting for a response, I turned and

ran up the stairs toward the roof. At the top, I burst through the metal door. Male grunts echoed across the barren landscape. Adrenaline surged. I rounded the corner to see Slade and Zeke knocking the shit out of each other.

As I rushed toward them, I was surprised that Slade was having so much trouble. Sure, he'd promised to wait for me to get there for the kill, but I hadn't expected him to follow through on it. Every assassin knows when you get an opening to finish the job, you take it. But Slade didn't even have a stake in his hand. Zeke was fighting, but he was also winded and scared. Slade should have had the advantage hands down.

I pulled my gun from my waistband and advanced. Slade pushed Zeke back against the low wall surrounding the roof. Slade knew I was there, because next thing I knew, he yelled, "Shoot him!"

Normally, I wouldn't have hesitated, but my hands shook and sweaty palms made my grip slippery. I didn't want to risk missing and clipping Slade by mistake. "Move!"

When Slade looked over his shoulder at me, Zeke clocked him on the side of the head and took off running again. My partner swept his feet under Zeke's legs, knocking the fat bastard to the ground. Then Slade jumped over and grabbed the gun from my hands. He spun and took a shot.

The bullet whizzed by a good foot from Zeke's head. He lurched off the ground and rammed his good shoulder into Slade. The assassin cursed and fell on his ass. Zeke loomed over him, but Slade still had the gun.

Now, I thought, now he'll get him.

Slade pulled the trigger. The bullet went wide again and lodged itself in an HVAC unit. My mouth dropped open; shocked he could miss such an easy shot.

Zeke, spurred on by adrenaline, ran toward the door—and me. Driven by pain and fear, he barreled right toward me. I bent my knees and pulled my spare gun from my waistband.

For one second, Zeke's face was a mask of rage barreling toward me. Then time slowed, and the gun in my slippery grip exploded. Blood burst from Zeke's right eye socket. His body jerked back, his arms going wide in forced surrender. He ignited before his body hit the rooftop.

I stood still for a moment as the shock of what I'd done soaked in. "I did it," I whispered. "I finally did it."

Slade groaned on the ground nearby. I walked over and gave him a hand up. "You okay?" I asked.

He nodded. "Sorry 'bout that," Slade said, motioning vaguely. "It's been a while since I shot a gun."

"No problem," I said, somewhat shakily. "At least we got him."

"You did good," he said. He gently pulled the gun from my steely grip. "You did real good."

I wiped my sweaty palms on my jeans. "Guess we'll need to call the sweepers to clean up this mess."

He nodded. "How's the faery?"

"Not good," I said. "But luckily Rolf decided to jump the gun and came to get her."

Just then, the door to the roof slammed open. Mischa exploded through it at full speed. When she saw the pile of ash smoldering on the ground, she yelled, "No! This was my kill."

"Day late and a dollar short as usual, Mischa." Slade flashed me a grin that made his normally harsh face look roguishly handsome.

She stamped her feet and punched the wall—a vampire temper tantrum. Pitiful.

Slade turned to me and slung his arm across my shoulder. "Come on, Sabina. Let's go celebrate your first kill."

∞

I couldn't sit still on the way home. By the time he turned into my neighborhood, Slade looked at me with a rueful smile. "I remember my first kill," he said wistfully.

Needing something to do to distract me from my restlessness, I turned to him. "Tell me about it."

He shrugged. "Not much to tell, really. The target was a low-level clerk for the Dominae. He'd cooked some books and siphoned a couple hundred thousand before anyone detected it. Easy kill. But I'll never forget how I felt after."

"Excited?"

He smiled, turning into my driveway. "More than that. The closest word I can think of is aroused." He punctuated the word by slamming the van into park.

"Yes," I said, looking him in the eye. "Aroused. That's the perfect word."

He watched me in the dark, saying nothing.

"Do you still feel that way after a kill?" I asked, licking my lips.

He answered with his mouth, but not with words. One second, he was on his side of the van, watching me with heat in his eyes. The next, he was on me. I welcomed the contact, reveling in another type of adrenaline. His fang scraped my lip, and he sucked on the sting, heightening the pain…and the pleasure.

We barely made it inside before the clothes came off. A small voice in the back of my head wondered if this was a mistake. After all, sex and business never mix well. But, another voice said, you're off the clock. The mission was successful, and it's time to celebrate.

I chose to listen to the latter voice and welcomed Slade's tongue in my mouth once again. His copper scent combined with the musk of exertion from the night's battle. He slammed me up against the wall and I felt the drywall give with the force of his thrusts. I wrapped my legs around his hips, meeting him thrust for thrust. He filled me thoroughly, but I wasn't content to let him have control.

He reached up and grabbed a handful of my hair. I jerked away and lowered my legs. I pushed him back roughly toward a dining room chair. Slade smiled and obeyed. He fell heavily onto it and pulled me down after him. My legs bracketing his hips, I dug my toes into the hardwood floor for a better grip. My nails dug into his shoulders, leaving small beads of blood I licked away. Slade groaned and urged me on with filthy whispers.

I'd had sex before, but that had been restrained, polite affairs with upper-class vampires who thought bagging a highborn mixed-blood would be an adventure. But behind Slade's tightly controlled façade lurked an animalistic lover. One spurred on by the excitement of the kill. My own internal beast rose to meet his and I gave him back as good as I got. Scratching, clawing, fucking until we were both left sweaty and spent on the cold floor.

∞

The next evening, I woke when the bed dipped. My eyes fluttered open. Slade sat on the edge of the bed, pulling on his boots. His clothes were on and his keys lay on the bed next to his hip.

"You're leaving?" I said.

"Got to go pick up our payment, but I'll be back."

"Cool," I said lamely. The muscles in my shoulders relaxed. It's not that I expected him to declare himself just because we'd screwed. But still. No one liked it when their partner dashed out the door after a night of hot, sweaty sex. "Fifty-fifty, right?" I joked.

He smiled. "You don't give up, do you?"

"You'll find I always get what I want," I said.

He leaned down and kissed me. Unlike the frenzied kisses last night, this one was long and slow. Tender. Almost like he was saying goodbye for more than a couple of hours. When he pulled away and smiled, I shook off the heavy feeling of foreboding. "Fifty-fifty it is."

"Excellent. When you get back, we'll celebrate."

For a split second, I thought I saw a shadow pass behind his hooded eyes. But then he patted my ass and rose. "It's a date. Be back soon."

I leaned back in the bed and listened to him leave. His footsteps on the hardwood floor. The click of the door closing. Then, a few moments later, the van's engine roaring to life.

I clenched my stomach muscles against the tickle of excitement. Everything was coming together for the first time in my life. I'd finally made my first kill. Now my grandmother would have to accept my competence.

And the fact I'd managed to finally outdo that bitch Mischa Petrov made the victory so much sweeter. The look on her face when she realized we'd beaten her was worth more to me than any monetary reward.

And what about Slade? Right then, Slade was a big question mark. A very sexy, intense question mark. I scooted down into the covers as a smile spread across my face.

Sure, the job didn't leave a lot of room for romance, but there was no reason we couldn't be friends with benefits. Using each other to work off the post-job glow, as it were. And who knew? Maybe more would grow. I allowed myself to daydream about us teaming up on more missions. He'd teach me everything he knew about being an assassin, and I'd reward him with hot, steamy sex. Seemed like a fair deal.

∞

By the next evening, my post-sex glow had turned into an inferno of anger. I slammed my fist into the table. "Where is he?" I demanded. All rational thought had flown out the window in the last twenty-four hours, but it wasn't until this moment that rage filled up the hollow place that logic had abandoned.

"Calm yourself," my grandmother snapped. "We don't know where he went."

When Slade failed to reappear the night before,

I'd spent the first hour in denial. Traffic, I'd reasoned. By the third hour, I'd paced a trough in my floor. By sunrise, after several unanswered phone messages, I'd gone into panic mode. What if something happened to him? Every now and then, even good assassins lost their luck and fell under the gun of a pissed-off friend or relative.

I'd called the Dominae headquarters just before sunrise, hoping they'd heard something. Tanith informed me Slade had come by to collect the payment as expected. She hadn't heard from him since, she said—not to worry.

After a sleepless day, my phone rang at about seven that night. I'd rushed to answer, convinced Slade was calling to explain. Instead, my grandmother commanded me to report to the compound ASAP. I'd driven over with dread pooling in my gut like tar.

When I arrived, my grandmother told me what they thought might have happened to Slade. I couldn't believe it.

"After you called last night, Tanith sent someone to check Slade's house. The signs of a hasty departure were unmistakable."

"But we don't know for sure he ran," I said, hating the desperate hope in my tone. "Maybe someone kidnapped him."

Tanith shook her head. "He also left this." She slid a note across the desk. As I read the letter, my dread morphed into black rage.

The note was addressed to the Dominae. The

content was short and to the point: "I can't do this anymore."

"How could he just disappear like that? Surely someone knows where he went," I said.

Tanith shook her head. "Sabina, Slade is one of our best assassins. He knows how to disappear when he wants to. He has more than a full night's head start, and for all we know, he's been planning this for a while."

I closed my eyes. I'd been so stupid. A foolish girl blinded by hero worship and eagerness to please. On that first night, Slade had said he had a lot riding on this mission. I saw now that he'd been planning to leave before I even entered the picture. He'd played me for three days, allowing me to think we were a team, when the truth was I was a pawn in his plan to cut and run.

He'd mentioned not seeing eye to eye with the Dominae. And when I'd asked him if he regretted killing anyone, he'd clammed up. Then there was the way he didn't get the job done with Zeke.

"Oh, shit," I said as the rest became clear.

"What?"

"Does Slade ever use guns?"

Tanith and Lavinia shared a confused glance. "Of course. He's an excellent marksman. Why?"

I closed my eyes and shook my head. "He told me he didn't like to use guns. He only carried stakes when we were together."

"That makes no sense," Tanith said.

"It makes perfect sense. Last night, he

deliberately missed Zeke twice. He all but forced me to carry out the kill."

"Why would he do that?" Lavinia asked.

"Don't you see? Slade lost his edge. That's why he ran. He said he couldn't take it anymore." I held up the note. "He used me to kill Zeke so he could collect the money and run."

"Wait—you made the kill?" Lavinia said. "Slade told me you froze and he had to finish the job."

Before this little revelation, I'd been hot with anger. Now, the blood in my veins became an ice floe. "Did he? And I'm sure you bought that, didn't you? Easier to believe I choked than to believe that Slade was playing you all for fools!"

"That's enough!" Lavinia yelled.

"You're right. It is enough. I will not be punished for Slade's choices. I carried out the mission as instructed. I want you to clear me for solitary kills." I thought about asking them to pay me, but that didn't matter anymore. I wasn't going to let Slade's duplicity screw me out of my chance to be a real assassin.

My grandmother stared me down with black eyes. I didn't flinch—didn't give her a hint of weakness to use as an excuse to deny me. Finally, she lowered her chin. "Fine. But you must promise to speak to no one about Slade's desertion. Is that clear?"

I jerked a nod. "Crystal."

"I'd hoped working with Slade would teach

you lessons about how to be a good assassin," Tanith said, shaking her head.

"Don't worry, Domina. The lesson Slade taught me was much more valuable than any he could have planned."

"And what might that be?" Lavinia said.

I shook my head and turned to go. They allowed me to leave without comment. But as I walked out of the room and saw the hostile faces of the Undercouncil, and those other vampires who saw me as nothing more than a mixed-blood, the lesson echoed through my head.

I'll always be better off alone.

∞

By the time I got home, my indignation had burned off, leaving the suffocating smoke of melancholy behind. I got out of my car and dragged my sorry ass up the sidewalk with my head hung low. It wasn't until I was almost on the porch that the feeling struck me that I was being watched.

I froze and looked around. The street was deserted and I didn't detect any life among the tall trees surrounding the house. A noise came from the shadows of the porch. I flicked my gaze in the direction. A small, traitorous part of my mind hoped to find Slade standing there. Instead, a pair of tiny eyes flashed from the darkness.

Hisss!

I blew out my breath and let my shoulders sag. "Oh, it's you." I stepped onto the porch, where Satan was sitting on my doormat.

The cat's head tilted. "Meow."

"Don't try apologizing. It's not going to work." I pulled out my keys and unlocked the door without looking at the furball. When I pushed the door in, I held out a foot to block the cat's entrance. It hissed and scratched at my boots. With a sigh, I grabbed Satan by the scruff of its neck.

Looking into the cat's eyes, I hardened my heart. It would be so easy to let the cat back inside. But I knew it was only a matter of time before Satan escaped again. I shook my head. No, better to end this now. I didn't have room in my life for anyone or anything. Certainly not for an ungrateful beast who shit all over my life before running away. "It's over, Satan," I said. "Don't come back."

I walked to the edge of the porch and set him below the step. The cat fell back on its butt and meowed up at me. I put my hands on my hips. "Go! Get out of here."

I flashed my fangs and hissed. The cat's hackles rose and he hissed before streaking toward the treeline.

After Satan was gone, I allowed myself to deflate. Going inside, I dropped my stuff on the floor and locked the door behind me. I leaned back against the door and closed my eyes. Silence surrounded me, pressing in on my skin.

Alone.

I told myself it was better this way. Life was a lot easier when you didn't trust anyone. Simpler. Simple was good. I looked around at the ruined sofa and the shit stains on my living room rug. I'd learned the hard way that opening myself up to trusting others was messy.

Pushing off the door, I went into my kitchen for a beer. I pulled back the tab and drank deeply. But the carbonation couldn't wash away the bitter taste on my tongue. When I lowered the beer, my gaze landed on the bag of cat food and the shiny bowls I'd bought for Satan.

I pursed my lips and tried to decide what to do with all the gear I'd bought. I could throw them away. But right then, an image of Satan with its hackles up rose in my mind. I thought about the notch out of its ear from fighting. I thought about the matted hair and the aggression. No wonder Satan had been so angry. The cat never found anyone it could trust, either.

My decision made, I filled one bowl with food and the other with water. Before I could second-guess myself, I snuck out the front door and stashed the food in the far corner of my porch. Then I went back inside, locked the door, and stood at the window.

Fifteen minutes later, an orange-tinted shadow appeared on the porch. Satan's steps were cautious. I held my breath and peeked through a miniscule slit in the blinds. The cat glanced at the door, as if expecting a trick. When I didn't jump out at it, it took a few more steps toward the food.

Then after a good long while, Satan reached the bowl, sniffed it experimentally, and then lost its battle against caution. The cat dove face first into the food and chowed down.

Smiling, I closed the blinds and left the cat to its feast.

I told myself that the food was just a peace offering. An apology of sorts for scaring the little shit earlier. But deep down, I knew I'd keep refilling that bowl as long as Satan kept appearing to eat it.

However, I'd never ever invite the cat into my house again. My life didn't have room for pets. As it turned out, Slade Corbin had taught me a valuable lesson, after all: Caring made you vulnerable.

Besides, I thought, turning out the lights, cats were the kind of pets mages kept. I chuckled at the thought. The day I started acting like a freaking mancy would be the day I summoned a demon to stake me in the heart with Applewood.

VIOLET
TENDENCIES

The Tit Crypt hadn't changed much over the years. The neon sign over the mausoleum-shaped building still featured a pair of breasts that throbbed with each blink of the lights. Letters under the enormous glowing rack warned passers-by this club was strictly members only. It didn't mention all the members were vampires.

"So, Sabina," Adam said, "Your friend isn't exactly into subtlety, is he?"

"With a name like 'Fang' was there any doubt?" I hefted a duffle bag onto my shoulder. Adam clenched the twin to my bag in his right hand.

"Okay," I said, "Everyone play it cool in there."

"Please," a voice came from inside the bag I held. "My middle name is 'Cool.'"

A female voice from Adam's bag responded, "You said your middle name was 'Hung.'"

"Whatever," I said. "Just remember to keep a low profile, okay? We don't want the Dominae to know we're in town yet. Just about the only thing we have going for us right now is the element of surprise."

Once the demons in the bags mumbled their agreement, we set out. Other than a couple of drunken vamps stumbling out the front door, the place looked tight. We skirted the front and made our way to the back of the building. Although, frankly, if we'd gone in the front door chances were good the patrons' eyes would have been on the strippers. But we didn't want to take any chances.

I banged on the heavy steel door in the alley behind the building. A couple of seconds later it opened to reveal six-foot-five inches of leather-clad vampire. Adam stiffened at my side. Couldn't blame him, really. In addition to his impressive size, Fang's scowl and full-sleeve tattoos of vampire pin-up girls gave him a decidedly threatening air.

"Hiya, Fang," I said, unable to contain my damn-it's-good-to-see-you smile.

"Come give me some sugar!" He hauled me up into his massive arms for a bear hug and a grope. I laughed and hugged him back.

Seeing Fang again brought back memories of the good old days—simpler times when I made my living killing vampires for the Dominae. Now I was one being hunted and the word "complicated" didn't begin to describe the shit-storm that was my life.

When he finally set me down, I turned to Adam, who watched the reunion with arms crossed and eyes narrowed.

"Adam, this is Fang. He owns this den of iniquity," I said. "And Fang, this is Adam, the mage friend I told you about."

The two males eyed each other, sharing terse nods and a white knuckled handshake. They might as well have whipped out their dicks for a little compare and contrast.

But, to their credit, this wasn't an average territorial, tough guy greeting. Each also had to weigh whether their mutual acquaintance with me meant they could trust each other. Mages and vampires weren't easy allies as a rule. Especially now with a war between the races all but inevitable.

Scratching noises came from inside my duffle bag, followed by an "Ahem!"

"Oh, right." I held up the bag. "And this is my demon minion, Giguhl."

Fang peeked into the panel on the side of the bag. A shadowed outline of a cat with huge, hairless ears appeared against the mesh. "Hey there, Mr. Kitty."

An evil hiss ripped through the air. Fang jerked his hand away and shot me a worried look.

"Um, Fang?" I said. "He's kind of sensitive about the cat thing."

Fang's eyes narrowed as he looked inside the bag again. "I'm sorry?"

"You should be, asshole," said the bitchy kitty.

I dropped the bag on the ground. A muffled yelp followed, along with a word that sounded suspiciously like "bitch." I shot Fang a lame smile and mumbled a quick apology. Then I motioned to Adam, who lifted his own bag obligingly.

"And this," I said, motioning to the small blinking eyes and beak just visible inside the bag, "is Valva."

Fang's smile froze. "Did you just say--"

"Vahhhl-va," the peacock purred from the carrier.

"Okay," he said slowly, eyeing the bag. "Why don't you and your "—he struggled for the proper word for a second before finally settling on—"friends come on in to my office."

I nodded and made to follow him in, but Adam put a hand on my arm. When I looked at him, he was frowning. "Are you sure we can trust this guy?"

I sighed. "Adam, do you really think I'd bring us here if I didn't?" I couldn't really blame the mage for his suspicion. But I wasn't any more interested in finding trouble here than he was. "Fang and I go way back. He's cool."

Adam jerked his head toward the door. "Lead the way then."

As we made our way toward Fang's office, the pulsing beat of the club's music made the walls throb. The noise made it unlikely Fang had overheard my hushed conversation with Adam.

And thank the gods for that—I didn't need to offend my only ally in Los Angeles.

Fang slung a heavy arm across my shoulders and led me to a doorway at the end of the hall. "Godsdamn it's good to see you!" His voice boomed over the music. "Didn't think I'd ever see you again after that trouble you got into with the Dominatrixes last month."

I smiled at the derogatory term for the Dominae. "Believe me, I didn't think I'd be back either."

He opened a door and flipped on the light. Fang's office was actually a storeroom with one metal desk and an ancient rolling chair shoved in a corner. The rest of the room contained shelves filled with jugs of baby oil, cases of toilet paper, and several kegs of beer. Through the crack in a door at the rear of the room, I spied a cot and some cleaning supplies. Probably for dealing with the oil slicks Fang's skanks left behind on the stage. It wasn't the Four Seasons, but it beat sleeping in the truck we'd boosted. If Fang let us stay there, that is.

"Um, Sabina?" Giguhl's plaintive voice came from inside the bag as I set it down on the floor.

"What?" I said, flashing Fang an apologetic smile.

"Can we switch back now?"

I sighed. "Hold on." To Fang, "Do you mind if I let the demons take their true forms? They've been stuck in these bags for a while." We'd flashed into L.A. using what Adam called "interspatial travel." It's kind of like the magical version of having Scotty beam us up, except with more nausea. Regardless, Adam insisted the demons travel in their animal forms since we'd need to be mobile the second we touched down in the City of Angels. Besides, a cat and peacock were easier to hide than a seven-foot-tall Mischief demon and his golden-skinned, blue-tailed Vanity demon girlfriend.

Fang shrugged. "Suit yourself."

Adam and I opened zippers and the cat and peacock emerged from their canvas cocoons. After some exaggerated stretching and whining about animal cruelty, they settled down enough for me say the incantation that allowed them to change forms.

A loud pop sounded in the small room, followed by two plumes of smoke—one green and the other blue—that smelled of rotten eggs. The stink cloud finally cleared enough to reveal the demons in all their naked glory. Fang stumbled back.

Obviously amused to see the big bad vamp's shock, Adam didn't even bother covering his shit-eating grin. Fang's fear was short-lived. Hard to be intimidated by two nude demons doing the pee-pee dance, I guess.

I threw a pair of sweatpants at Giguhl and a long T-shirt to Valva. I'd learned the hard way to carry extra clothes in a backpack for them. The switch between forms always resulted in exposed demon junk. Not pretty.

Giguhl pulled on his pants quickly. "It's an emergency."

"Me too," Valva's high-pitched voice came from inside the t-shirt as she slipped it over her head.

Fang's eyes tracked the demons' every move. "Bathrooms are down the hall."

"I'll go with them," Adam said. I nodded my thanks, grateful for a second to talk to Fang without an audience. The trio disappeared and shut the door behind them.

Once we were alone, Fang blew out a breath. "What the hell have you gotten yourself into, Sabina?"

Between hunting down my grandmother, who'd kidnapped my twin and trying to avert a war, not to mention the crazy secret cult who wanted to kill me before I could accomplish that goal, I wasn't really clear on which drama Fang was taking issue with. "I'm afraid you're going to have to be more specific here, dude."

"I know you're on the Dominae's shit list, but surely you didn't have to resort to slumming with mages and demons."

His venom set me on edge. "Those are my friends, Fang. If you have a problem with them you have a problem with me."

He held up a hand. "Wait. I'm sure they're fine if you trust them. It's just, if the Dominae find out I was harboring both you and a mage, I'd be good as dead."

I sighed. "Look, I'm sorry to drag you into this. I just didn't know where else to go. The Dominae will be watching hotels and the regular haunts. Hell, they probably already upped the price on my head."

"Since you mentioned it…" Fang walked to the desk and picked up a stack of papers. "I know you said you were back in town to find someone, but you're not going to get very far with these circulating." He handed me the first sheet from the stack. "They've plastered these all over the city."

My own face looked up at me with a sly smile. I remembered the picture had been taken at a party at my old friend Ewan's bar. That night we'd been drinking hard, and Ewan had captured a rare unguarded moment. Little did I know then that a year later he'd be dead and I'd be on the Dominae's hit list.

The flier claimed I was missing and feared kidnapped. It also said my family was offering ten thousand dollars for information leading to my safe return.

Acid filled my stomach and my fangs ground together. "Shit." Normally, when the Dominae put prices on vampires' heads they spread the word quietly among the fanged community. But now, they'd cleverly recruited humans into helping them too. And, of course, the irony of claiming I'd been the one kidnapped was a little extra dig. I crumpled the paper in my palm and silently promised my twin, Maisie, I'd find her and make Lavinia pay.

Painfully.

To Fang, I said, "Only ten grand? I think I'm insulted."

He wasn't impressed by my bravado. "If I were you, I'd forget whoever you're looking for and get the hell out of Dodge."

I shook my head. "I can't. They have my sister."

"You have a sister?" His eyes widened. "Is she as good lookin' as you?"

I appreciated him trying to lighten the mood, so I forced a small smile. "Actually, she looks exactly like me." While he digested this with a whistle, I carried on. "The Dominae kidnapped her from the mage compound in New York last night."

"And you figure they've got her at the Dominae estate in Malibu?" When I nodded, he continued. "Damn, Sabina, good luck. Between the flier and the Dominae's security, you're gonna need a miracle to get her back."

I nodded to indicate the truth of that statement. "I know, but I've got to try."

He sighed and crossed his arms. "How can I help?"

"I was kind of hoping you could put us up for a couple of nights."

Fang sucked air through his teeth. "I don't know, Sabina. You know I'd do almost anything for you, but—"

I held up a hand. "The last thing I want to do is put you or your girls in danger, but you have my word we'll be careful not implicate you in anything. We just need a place to crash. Otherwise you won't even know we're here."

Fang relaxed a tad, and I was convinced he was about to relent when Adam burst through the door. The heavy bass of the club's music had been muffled until that moment, but now it flooded into the room with a vengeance.

One look at the expression on Adam's face and my heart skipped a beat. "We've got a problem."

"Oh shit," I said. "What did Giguhl do now?"

He shook his head. "Not Giguhl. Valva."

∞

Cat calls and whistles echoed down the hallway—loud enough to be heard over the ear-bleeding volume of Axl Rose welcoming us to the jungle. Someone really needed to talk to Fang's DJ about updating the playlist.

Giguhl stood in the shadowed hallway. Just beyond him, an archway opened up into the club. The demon's eyes were locked on the stage. His posture was stiff and his fists clenched like rocks at his sides.

I skidded to a halt next to him with Adam and Fang behind me. "G, where is—" My voice trailed off as I followed his glare to the stage.

"Oh shit!" I yelped.

Apparently, I needed to have a little chat with the Vanity demon about the meaning of the phrase "low profile." It certainly didn't involve spinning on a stripper pole fully nude. Yet, that's exactly what she was doing.

Her golden skin might have looked like a bodysuit to the unfocused eye, but if you looked long enough it was hard to miss the two pert, gilded nipples and a bush that sparkled like Christmas tinsel.

"Does someone want to explain how the hell this happened?" I demanded, turning on Adam and Giguhl.

Giguhl was too busy glaring at the males waving dollar bills at his true love to answer. Adam wouldn't meet my eyes, but mumbled, "She snuck out while Giguhl was taking his sweet time in the john."

"Shut it, mancy. It's not my fault magical travel gives me stress diarrhea."

Just then, a gasp rippled through the crowd. Onstage, Valva had unfurled her peacock tail in all its blue, feathery glory.

"She's amazing," Fang said with dollar signs in his eyes. "They love her."

I shot him a glare. "How long do you think it's going to be before word gets back to the

Dominae you've got yourself a new demon stripper?"

That got his attention. "Get her off there. Now!"

I rolled my eyes. "If we run out there and make her get off the stage it'll cause more of a scene than any of us want."

"Um, guys? Whatever we do we better make it quick," Adam began, nodding at the gaggle of pissed vamp strippers gathering on the edge of the stage, "Or this place is going to turn into cat-fight-city."

Valva ignored the venomous stares of the red-headed, pasties-wearing posse and continued to taunt and tease the males at the foot of the stage into a frenzy. The pile of dollars at her feet was quickly growing into a mountain.

I opened my mouth to tell Fang to cut the music, so we could plead technical difficulties. But right then, a stripper in assless chaps made her move. One second, Valva was executing a jaw dropping one-legged spin on the pole, and the next, Chaps had her by the hair and was dragging the demon across the stage. The gaggle of strippers fell on her like vultures on road kill, much to the excitement of the crowd of vampire males, who sensed imminent blood sport.

I cursed and ran toward the stage. It's not that I worried Valva would get hurt. As a demon, she could hold her own. Instead, I worried that in addition to starting a riot in Fang's club, I'd also be responsible for his girls being harmed—an offense he would never forgive.

As I made my way through the crowd, customers started taking sides in the stripper battle. Suddenly fists, chairs and even some bodies flew through the air like shrapnel.

Behind me, Adam and Giguhl waded into the melee, shouting to each other over the din. I elbowed a couple of male vamps in the face on my way, but didn't stop to engage. My sole goal was to get to the stage and stop Valva before things escalated from what-the-hell to oh-shit.

Somehow, Adam and I reached the pile-up of boobs and fists at the same time. I turned to yell for Giguhl. He was most likely to be able to handle Valva. But my yell turned into a yelp as someone grabbed a fistful of my hair from behind.

I grabbed the hand and held it close to my scalp to lessen the pain and twisted around to deliver a fist to a taut, glittered midsection. My opponent wore a pair of pasties shaped like stars, a green spangled G-string, and a pair of Lucite heels with flashing lights in the sole. But what she lacked in clothing, she made up for in fury.

If this had been a run-of-the-mill mortal stripper, she'd already be dead. But Fang's vampettes were some tough bitches who liked to fight dirty. Too bad I didn't remember that before the harpy scored my face with her neon-green dragon lady nails.

"Godsdammit!" I yelled, sidestepping just in time to avoid the stomp of her platform heel. I hooked my ankle around her knee. She slipped and slammed to the stage easily thanks to the baby oil slick.

I turned to find Adam with six strippers clinging to him like big-breasted leeches. Gods love him, he tried to look like he wasn't enjoying himself. But he hadn't zapped any of them either. I grabbed one by the arm and flung her away. Nearby, Valva picked up Assless Chaps and threw her across the room. Four male vamps broke her fall and toppled like bowling pins.

"Valva!" I yelled. "Stop!"

She flashed me a smile. Right then, Guns N Roses gave way to the opening chords of Heart's "Barracuda." Valva ignored me and executed a swan dive off the stage. The men in the audience roared in approval as she began to crowd surf. A trio of strippers noted her escape and started fighting customers in an attempt to reach their prey.

Adam and I stood on stage, panting. In horror, we watched the bar devolve into a bare-breasted brawl. Fang and his bouncers attempted to hack their way through the mosh pit of doom. My old friend glared at me through the smoke and projectiles with an expression that promised retribution. Looked like our welcome had been officially revoked.

As if the scene wasn't enough of a clusterfuck,

Giguhl dove off the stage and wrecking-balled his way into the crowd. Vampires flew through the air like discarded trash. Totally oblivious to the chaos she'd created—or maybe because of it—Valva couldn't have looked happier.

"Valva!" Giguhl yelled, punching a rough-looking male vamp in the face.

I grabbed Adam's arm. "Can't you do some spell or something to stop this?"

He ran hand through his hair. "What do you want me to do, Sabina? He's your demon."

Oh. Right. "Giguhl!" I screamed. "I command you to stop!"

Giguhl's fist paused mid-strike. His arm shook as he strained to deliver the blow. But my minion couldn't deny a direct order. Probably, I'd hear an earful about this later, but right then all I cared about was stopping the fight.

I jumped off the stage and pushed my way toward the action. Unfortunately, a few of the patrons mistook me for a stripper. But I endured the gropes and leers because they were easier to get through than fists and kicks.

Finally, I managed to reach the horde of vamps parading the demon around the bar. "Valva! Get down from there right now!"

She ignored me. Unlike Giguhl, Valva wasn't officially my minion. That honor belonged to my sister, Maisie. Which meant, Valva didn't have to do anything she didn't want to do.

Going for a more direct approach, I pushed a

guy out of the way and grabbed her leg. I yanked on her leg, but the males were having none of it. Someone grabbed me from behind and before I knew it, the world tilted and gravity reversed itself. They lifted me right up next to Valva.

"Hi, Sabina!" she said. "Isn't this great?"

Before I could answer, the crowd surfed us over to the bar. Valva landed gracefully on the surface, blowing kisses and flicking her flirtatiously. One of the males carrying me decided to grab a handful of my left ass cheek before helping me onto the bar. Frustrated and pushed beyond patience, I slammed my fist into his nose. The cartilage gave with a satisfying crunch.

"Hey!" he yelled, dropping me. I landed on the filthy carpet with a thud. The guy loomed over me. Blood coated his fierce scowl. But then his expression changed from anger to recognition. "Wait, aren't you—"

"Fire!" The shout broke through the chaos. I looked up in time to see the bar explode into flames. A flash of gold flew by my head—Valva making a hasty retreat from her smoldering impromptu stage. I had no idea how she'd managed to set the thing on fire, but I had a more pressing issue to worry about at the moment.

I leapt to my feet, pushing the angry male aside. Obviously, the situation was way beyond diffusing. Time to just cut our losses and disappear. I spun to locate Adam and slammed into an unmovable object. One with an impossibly broad chest, a leather vest, and tattoos.

I looked up slowly and cringed when my gaze reached his face. Fang's expression wasn't so much angry as apocalyptic. He grabbed my arms. "What the fuck have you done?"

"Fang, I—"

The heat and flash of the fire caught my eye. Flames licked across the floor, searing a path to the stage. On the platform, eight or ten vampire strippers continued their bloody battle. Apparently Fang's strippers had some unresolved personal issues because they were wailing on each other, using any weapons at their disposal. Chairs crashed into heads. Thongs became garrotes. And jugs of baby oil—

"Oh shit!" My gaze flew back to Fang's face. "Is baby oil flammable?"

He squinted hard. "Huh—"

Too late. The flames already reached the base of the stage. "We need to help them!"

Either he couldn't hear me or he was so enraged he chose not to listen, but Fang's grip tightened and his fangs flashed ominously. A flash of light and a burst of heat exploded through the club. The stink of singed hair and broiled skin brought bile to my throat. And the screams. Terrible, terrible screams.

Looking directly at the stage-turned-pyre was almost too horrible. Looking like ghouls with melted wigs and blackened skin, the burning stripper danced around like scorched marionettes. Still, shock kept me rooted to the spot.

Fang burst into action, tossing me to the side as he leapt toward the bonfire, shouting for water as he ran. I went the other direction, intent on finding Adam and the others. I didn't get far before I saw Giguhl running in my direction with Valva in his arms. Her expression resembled that of a toddler about to throw an epic tantrum.

"Adam?"

Giguhl jerked his head toward the inferno that used to be the bar. "Over there!"

I nodded and took off, yelling, "Stay here!"

I hoped the demon could hear me over the yells of those who were trying to fight the fire and the screams of those trying to escape it. As I passed the group trying to help, I saw Fang yelling orders. He looked up as I passed and the hatred in his once-friendly eyes made my stomach contract.

Adam's golden-brown head should have been easy to spot among all the red-headed vampires. But the thick haze of smoke clawed at my eyes. Climbed down into my lungs. I couldn't see anything through the choking and the tears.

Rough hands grabbed me from behind. I spun into a crouch, ready to fight. Adam tilted his head and raised an eyebrow in greeting. Instead of witty comments or snarky asides, he grabbed my hand and hauled me back to the demon.

"Praise Asmodeus," Giguhl said. "Can we leave now?"

The mancy glanced at me for confirmation. I looked at the fire. At the soot-covered faces. At the flames dancing over smoldering bodies. "We should stay and help them."

"Red," Adam sighed. "Normally I'd agree but there's no chance now that the Dominae won't hear about this—or your involvement. We need to get the hell out of here before they find us."

Electricity flashed through my veins. Considering I'd cost Fang his beloved club, I wouldn't put it past my old friend to go to the Dominae himself and tell him we were back in town himself. Guilt swelled in my midsection like acid. But I nodded anyway.

Adam put his arms around us. Started chanting.

The pressure began in my solar plexus.

The doors to the club burst open. The fire rushed toward the fresh oxygen. Then a dozen figures dressed in black ducked into the club.

My heart stopped. Their red hair and the golden Fleur-de-lis insignias on their chests identified these new arrivals as Dominae guards.

"Mancy!" I yelled, urging Adam on. He didn't respond. Just frowned and focused harder on calling the magic.

"Sabina Kane!" Guns pointed in our direction. "Freeze in the name of the Dominae!"

Magic rushed through me like static electricity,

making the hair on my arms prickle. "Ready!"

Unbearable pressure.

"Aim!"

Wind whipped up around us.

"Fire!"

Pop—we were gone.

∞

An eternal instant later, my ears popped and my body landed on something springy. A heavy mass thumped next to me followed by a loud groan. Two more thuds echoed nearby. Fighting against the nausea and dizziness, I forced my eyes open.

Beside me, Adam pushed himself up on his elbows and frowned down at me. "That was way too close for comfort."

I licked my lips and tried to unscramble my brain. "Huh?"

"Are you okay?" His hand ran over my arms and torso, as if checking for wounds. I took a minute to enjoy his tactile inspection. But memory of the debacle at Fang's intruded, ruining any enjoyment I was getting out of Adam's nearness.

"I'm okay." I rubbed my nose in a futile effort to remove the lingering odor of burnt sequins and charred skin.

"You're sure?"

I nodded. I didn't like that we'd basically run

away from a mess of our own making, but since our only other choice was to hang around waiting to either be retaliated against by Fang or captured by the Dominae or... Well, let's just say that narrowed the options down considerably. "Where are we?"

He pulled away. The cool night air replaced his warmth. Standing, he gestured up with a wry smile. "Look for yourself."

I glanced up to where he pointed and blinked. Several tall white letters loomed over our heads. "The Hollywood sign?"

"I wasn't sure where else to go." He shrugged. "This seemed like a safe enough place for us to regroup." He held out a hand to pull me up. The momentum brought me back into contact with his body. Knowing the mage, he was doing it on purpose. Not that I minded, but it wreaked havoc on my ability to concentrate.

I stepped away and wiped my scraped and dirty hands on my jeans. Mostly I was fine, except where the rough landing bruised my ass. The demons, however, hadn't fared so well. They still hadn't moved.

I knelt next to Giguhl and listened for breathing. Big mistake. A steady diet of Cheese Doodles and catnip didn't make for the sweetest breath. But at least he was breathing. I glanced at Adam, who'd given Valva the same treatment. He gave me a thumb's up and I released the air I hadn't realized I'd been holding.

Now that I was sure they hadn't been injured, I relaxed. When we'd flashed into the city earlier that night they'd been disoriented but recovered quickly—Giguhl's stress diarrhea notwithstanding. But I guess two rounds of interspatial transportation in one night had taken its toll on them.

A groan grabbed my attention. I looked down to see Giguhl's eyelids squeeze tight for a moment before popping open. But the bright light overhead made his vertical pupils dilate. "Are we dead?"

"Nope. No thanks to your girlfriend."

Giguhl swallowed and sat up slowly. When he looked over and saw Valva still passed out, he let out a little yelp. "Valva?" He grabbed her chin and shook her. "Is she okay?"

Her lids snapped open. "Hi, honey!" she said in a breezy tone completely at odds with the situation.

"Hi, honey?" he roared. "Don't 'hi, honey' me!"

She frowned. "What's wrong, sugar buns?"

Giguhl's goat eyes widened impossibly. "What's wrong? How can you even ask that? You almost got us killed!"

Her golden lips went from a frown to a full-on pout. The bottom lip began to tremble. I rolled my eyes, recognizing feminine wiles when I saw them. "But I didn't mean to. Everything was fine until those *trampires* tried to stop me."

"Valva," Adam said, "What were you thinking getting up on stage in the first place?"

She shrugged her golden shoulders. "I couldn't help it."

"Bullshit," Giguhl said. "You couldn't wait to get out there and shake your sweet ass for all those blood suckers."

She blinked. "But I'm a Vanity demon," she said as if it explained everything.

"Like that excuses it?" Giguhl threw up his claws in frustration.

Pretty tears started to fall from her violet eyes. "I couldn't help it," she sobbed. "I swear."

"Giguhl," I said quietly. "Give her a break." Don't get me wrong. I was angry at her too, but I was shocked to hear Giguhl talk to her that way. Ever since the demons' eyes met across a bloodstained fight ring, it had been love at first sight. But now—

"Oh please." Giguhl scoffed. "No female of mine is allowed to act like a common tramp in public."

I cringed at his Cro-Magnon tone. Looked like the shine had worn off their sparkly new love.

Valva's tears dried up fast. She advanced on Giguhl, her golden hands clenched into fists and her blue-feathered tail twitching. She poked a finger into Giguhl's chest. "You listen here, buddy. I am no one's property. I'll shake my ass for whoever I want wherever I want."

"Okay, everyone needs to relax," Adam said,

approaching the pair. The demons ignored him.

"Is that right?" Giguhl growled, getting into Valva's face.

"I'm sick and tired of your clinging! I need some space."

Adam tried to get between the demons. "Valva, you don't mean that." The demons moved closer, edging Adam out of their space completely. He looked at me. "A little help here?"

I held up my hands and shook my head. Refereeing a demon lovers' spat was so not my area. "Just let them work it out." Adam pressed his lips together and looked to the sky for patience.

Giguhl crossed his arms across his massive chest. His eyes narrowed. "You want space? Why don't you just go back to Irkalla then?"

"Maybe I will," she said, poking him again. "At least I'm appreciated there."

"Valva," I said, finally moving in. Now that talk had turned to her leaving it was time for me to step in. "We appreciate you."

"No you don't." She turned on me. "You're bossy and you have split ends." She pointed at Adam. "You know what I'm talking about. Tell her!"

Adam lifted his hands and backed away, as if retreating from a ticking time bomb. "I've never noticed any split ends."

"Please, you know she's a bitch. Ordering us about like we're her slaves." She ran a hand over her peacock blue hair. "Besides, she's totally jealous of me."

"Hey!" I said, ignoring the ridiculous accusation. "Need I remind you that you and Giguhl are my minions? It's kind of my job to tell you what to do."

Valva laughed. "Giguhl's your minion. Maisie's my master. Or she was, at least."

I put my hands on my hips. This chick's attitude was grating on my last damned nerve. I also didn't appreciate her use of the past tense in relation to my sister. "Right. Maisie. Remember her? She's the one whose possibly being tortured while you waste all our time with your fucking temper tantrum."

"Oh please. You're all so fucking whiney. The only reason I chose to be her minion was to get out of going back to Irkalla."

My mouth fell open. "What do you mean you 'chose' her?"

"That's right, bitches. It was my choice. I just let you think it was destiny or whatever because it was easier." She snorted. "Boy was that a mistake. I thought staying here would be an adventure. But I'd rather be damned to the Pit of Despair than deal with your lame asses for one more second."

Giguhl's posture went stony. "What about me?" his voice was quiet but fire lurked in the subtext.

She shrugged. "I thought you'd be a fun lay."

Valva waggled her pinky at Giguhl. "What a joke."

My chest clenched for Giguhl. "You bitch."

"Pot. Kettle. Black," she enunciated slowly. "I'm so out of here."

Light burst through the area, momentarily blinding me. Brimstone smoke filled my nose. I blinked rapidly and finally saw wisps of black smoke snaking through the air where Valva used to stand.

My jaw gaping, I looked around at the guys. "What the hell?"

Adam's eyes were saucer-huge. "How did she just do that?"

Giguhl didn't answer. He just glared at the spot where she'd stood moments before. A muscle worked in his jaw.

I approached slowly, unsure how any show of comfort might be received. "G?" I whispered. "Are you okay?"

As if he'd forgotten our presence altogether, his head snapped up. His eyes had a wild look I'd only seen in the fighting ring. I held up my hands. "Hey, it's just me."

He shook himself, like a dog after a particularly objectionable bath. "Hey." He sounded disoriented, as if waking from a long nap. "What's up?"

I glanced from the corner of my eye at Adam. He just shrugged.

"Are you going to be okay?"

"What? Valva?" He waved a claw through the air. "Sure. No big deal."

I frowned at him. "Are you sure? She was kind of harsh."

"Sabina, I'm fine. She obviously wasn't the demon I thought she was. I'm better off without her."

"Okay," I said slowly. "Well, if you need to talk or whatever, I'm here." I said this clumsily, totally out of my depth when it came to offering emotional support to the broken hearted.

"Yep, thanks." With that, he turned and walked over to a boulder perched on the hill. He lifted the huge thing like a mortal might have lifted a heavy crate. Raising it over his head, his muscles strained for a moment. Then he launched the rock like a shot put.

The boulder flew so far, my eyes lost sight of it in the inky night sky. Several seconds later, a muted crash rose from deep in the canyon below. A dog's bark echoed through the night, followed by a single pinpoint of light igniting in a distant window.

"Whoops," Giguhl said.

The corner of my mouth twitched. "Feel better?"

He sucked in a lungful of air that expanded his chest. On the exhale, he roared so loud I had to check and see if my ear was bleeding. When the primal scream finally cut off, Giguhl smiled. "Now I feel better."

Adam removed his hands from his ears. "Um, maybe this isn't the best time to ask this question, but does anyone know how in the hell Valva managed to flash out of here like that?"

I shrugged my shoulders. "I was kind of hoping you'd know." I turned to Giguhl. "I thought only the mage who controlled the demon could send them back to Irkalla."

Adam nodded. "Right."

"It's because she's not a normal demon." Bitterness dripped from Giguhl's tone.

I frowned, trying to decide if he was serious or if it was the heartbreak talking. "What do you mean?"

He shrugged. "That rule only applies to your average *Shedim* demon."

Adam seemed to be following Giguhl's cryptic remarks better than me. His eyes widened. "Wait, she's a *Lilitu*?"

Giguhl nodded solemnly. "Yep."

"Wait," I said. "Can someone fill me in please?"

Giguhl offered the explanation. "There's two types of demons. Those that existed before time—the *Shedim*. No one really knows where we came from, but we know we've existed before Lilith fled the Garden of Eden and shacked up with Asmodeus."

I nodded. I'd never heard the word *Shedim*, but I knew enough of the origin stories to follow along. "Okay."

"The *Lilitu* are the demons who are direct descendants of Lilith and Asmodeus," Adam said.

"A bigger bunch of snooty demons you'll never meet," Giguhl added. "They think because they're royalty and shit that they're special. Even though the *Shedim* have been around eons longer."

I processed all this. "So what you're saying is that the Lilitu can move between the realms and the Shedim can't—without magical aid that is."

"Exactly," Giguhl said. "They usually don't come here, though. They're so privileged in Irkalla they don't usually bother with mortal concerns."

I raised a hand. "Does it bother anyone else that Valva is Lilith's daughter and we didn't know it?"

"I knew it," Giguhl said. "I just didn't think it mattered."

I raised my hands in frustration. "Of course it matters." Some people believed I was some sort of Chosen, prophesized by Lilith to unite all the dark races. So, the fact Valva might have been sent by the dark goddess to spy on me or whatever was information I could have used."

"Actually," Adam jumped in, "it may not. Lilith and Asmodeus have been popping out demons for millennia. Right, Giguhl?"

The demon nodded. "I'd guess they have about 100 billion kids, give or take."

"And think about it," Adam said. "Lenny

summoned Valva to fight Giguhl. Damara orchestrated all that by herself as far as we know."

He was right. Damara had been working for the Caste of Nod, who wanted me dead. She'd tried to get me killed, but when that didn't work, she blackmailed Lenny to have one of his demons kill Giguhl.

"It's not out of the realm of possibility that Lilith orchestrated it," I said.

"I don't know," Adam said. "It's kind of a stretch. Besides, she might have been a bitch, but she wasn't exactly a mastermind." He cringed and shot Giguhl an apologetic look. "Sorry, G."

Giguhl waved a claw. "Don't worry about it. Her lack of depth was one of the things I liked best about her." His shoulders slumped.

Time to change the subject before he demanded ice cream and a chick flick marathon. "Okay, now that we've figured that minor mystery out, we've got a bigger issue."

"Right," Adam said. "The Dominae."

I took a deep breath and thought about our options. My instinct was to go underground for a few days until the heat died down. But I was frankly tired of the Dominae having the upper hand. If we wanted to succeed, we'd need to do something unexpected. Something bold.

"Before we move on to that," Giguhl said. "I have something to say."

Adam and I both looked up from our musings.

"If I hadn't forced her on your guys none of this would have happened. I'm sorry my selfishness put us in this position."

I frowned. I so wasn't used to Giguhl going all sincere on me. "It's not your fault. She had us all fooled." I patted him on the arm. "But it's in the past now. We need to get our heads back in the game and figure out what our next move is now that the Dominae know we're here."

Giguhl shot me a grateful look. "Thanks, Sabina. You're a good friend."

My cheeks heated at his praise. "Don't get used to it," I said. "I'll be bossing you around again in no time."

"If I can add a wrinkle to things," Adam said. "We also need to figure out where we're spending the day." He nodded toward the horizon. The dark edges of night were already easing into the muted pinks of dawn.

"You two figure that out while I focus on this Dominae issue," I said. Two sets of raised eyebrows greeting my command. "Please."

I looked out over the city, which spread out below us like a blanket of lights. Somewhere to the west of us, the Dominae compound crouched on a cliff overlooking the Atlantic. I knew from memory that the security in the compound was impenetrable. Used to be, I could walk right in with the right passwords. But now, the place might as well have been Fort Knox. Too bad Lavinia rarely left the compound or we could have just planned an ambush.

I stilled. Lavinia never left the compound, but the other Dominae did. Tanith and Persephone handled most of the night-to-night business.

"Hey?" I called. "What day is it?"

"Let's see … " Adam looked up as he mentally counted days. "Monday? No, wait, it's Tuesday by now."

A smile spread across my lips. "Perfect."

The males frowned at me for a moment before resuming their discussion about the best place to crash. I took a moment to weigh the insanity of my new plan with the possible outcomes. Once I was sure it was our best option, I held up a hand. "Hey guys," I said, interrupting their debate over where we'd spend the day after the sun came up. "Anyone in the mood for a little kidnapping and extortion?"

RUSTED
VEINS

OCTOBER 27

Some cities are naturally holiday cities. London is a Christmas city. Paris is a Valentine's Day city. And no place in the world is a Halloween city more than New Orleans.

Maybe I feel that way because my first introduction to the Big Easy happened over Halloween a few years ago. Back then I'd headed there to find my twin sister who'd been kidnapped by our psychotic grandmother, Lavinia. Now the grandmother was dead, Maisie was the leader of the underworld, and I was the leader of all the Dark Races in the corporeal world and had made the Big Easy home. Life was funny like that sometimes.

Or maybe it was that New Orleans always felt like a liminal space, where the veil between the living and the dead was gossamer thin. Often, walking down the streets of Faubourg Marigny or through one of the infamous Cities of the Dead, you could almost swear that the veil didn't exist at all. It seemed the Big Easy, more than any other town in America, had long ago come to terms with its mortality, and its humans reveled in how close they danced with death. As an immortal, I found myself drawn to the ironic and inevitable sense of life their knowledge of death gave the city.

Yeah, a lot of people associate New Orleans with Fat Tuesday, a time of excess and gluttonous revelry. But one could argue that Mardi Gras was just one day and the celebrations leading up to it lasted a month, but every other day in New Orleans was Halloween.

Most of the Dark Races, like mages and the fae, call Halloween "Samhain," and it was just around the corner when I returned to my beloved city after an extended trip to Europe. As the head of the Dark Races Cabinet, I had to travel whenever a major conflict broke out between the different species of non-human beings anywhere in the world. This particular trip had taken me to Scotland to mediate a problem between a community of faeries and a family of vampires who wanted to move into a sacred faery ring. After that, I'd swung through Italy and Spain for summits with various subcouncils over matters relating to everything from territory rights for the Strega covens in Rome to some new feeding laws the vampires in Barcelona wanted passed.

When I returned home on October 27, I'd been looking forward to spending time with my main squeeze, Adam Lazarus, a seriously hot mage who I'd somehow convinced to love me. Instead, I'd gotten called into a special session of the council by the heads of all the Dark Races in America.

Don't get me wrong, uniting the Dark Races into a period of everlasting peace is great and all, but it's also kind of…annoying. Diplomacy doesn't exactly come naturally to me, and it's especially difficult when I have to play mediator between a pissed-off werewolf and a stubborn fae monarch.

"Faeries don't own the fucking Blue Ridge Mountains," growled Michael Romulus, Alpha of the New York pack. He sat at one end of the table and Queen Maeve sat at the other, facing off like two gunslingers.

"Maybe not, but you weres shouldn't be allowed to colonize anywhere you damned well please," Queen Maeve shot back.

"Guys," I said, "if you'll stop yelling, I'm sure we can come up with some sort of mutually beneficial compromise here." I mentally cursed my sister, Maisie, who was stuck in Irkalla dealing with a vampire ghost uprising and couldn't come help me play mediator. We technically ruled the council together, but normally I took point on issues with the living, while she handled the drama of the dead.

"Fat chance," Michael said. "I know how things work on this cabinet."

"What's that supposed to mean?" I asked.

"It's no secret that you're biased toward the fae."

I frowned at him like he'd lost his damned mind. Mike and I had had our moments in the past, but to outright accuse me of prejudice was insane. Still, I avoided the whole "we're all equals here" speech because that wasn't exactly true. The heads of each race may have a vote, but in the end my word was law.

"You're out of line, Romulus. If you want your request to be taken seriously, you need to drop the bullshit."

A muscle in his jaw tightened. "Screw this." His chair hit the ground with a crash. He stormed away from the table and out the door. In his wake, the echo of the slammed door reverberated through the chamber.

Everyone was silent for two heartbeats. Until Queen Maeve decided to speak.

"Werewolves are so touchy."

"Shut the hell up, Maeve," Rhea said. As the leader of the mage Hekate Council, Rhea didn't have a stake in the outcome of the land rights debate, but that didn't mean she didn't have an opinion. "You have no good reason for refusing to allow that pack on your lands."

The Queen's mouth dropped open. "How

dare you, mage!"

"No, Maeve, how dare *you*?" I said, my voice threaded with steel. "You might treat your courtiers with this type of disrespect, but I'll be damned if I let you cause hostility on my council because your mother never taught you to share."

"I didn't have a mother." Her mouth puckered. "I sprung fully formed from a peat bog."

I rolled my eyes. "Regardless, you've been alive, what, four thousand years?"

"Five thousand," she said in a haughty tone.

"Might as well be five, period," I shot back, "because you're acting like a child."

If it had been spring, Queen Maeve would have looked like a child and been even more prone to tantrums than usual. But as it happened, it was autumn, which meant the monarch was in her "mother" guise. As a demigoddess, she cycled through each season of womanhood—child, maiden, mother, and crone—each year. This evening, she looked like a human female in her prime. She wore the jewel tones of autumn and her long hair was bound in a wreath of acorns and ruby leaves.

While she sputtered her outrage, I held up a hand. "The Blue Ridge Mountains are large enough for your kingdom and one small pack of werewolves, isn't it?"

"That's not the point," she said. "We claimed those mountains when the Dark Races began the great migration from Europe. Just as the mages stake their claim on New York and the bloodsuckers—"

Nyx, the leader of the American vamps, and therefore one of the most politically powerful vampires in existence, took exception to the derogatory term for her race and cleared her throat.

The Queen spared the vamp an annoyed glance. "Just as the Lilim did in Los Angeles. My point is, why is it okay for our territory to be invaded by the weres when you know damned well they'd need special permission to settle in mage or vamp territory?"

"Asking for permission is exactly what Mike's doing. And P.S., Orpheus had no qualms about allowing the werewolves to settle in Manhattan decades ago."

"Yes, well, look where Orpheus's permissiveness got him."

"That's enough," Rhea snapped. Her outburst wasn't a surprise seeing how the deceased former leader of the mages had been her best friend and rumored lover.

"All right," I said. "Let's table this discussion for tonight. But I expect a resolution before Samhain."

The queen pursed her lips and crossed her arms. "Tell that to him."

"I intend to. Now, is there any new business?"

Several heads wisely shook to decline my

invitation. I rapped my gavel on the table. "Then this meeting is adjourned."

∞

After the council meeting, I left the chambers and all but ran across the grounds toward the house to find Adam before anyone could distract me with more diplomatic drama. I found him in the library on the first floor of our Garden District mansion. Even though it wasn't that cold out, a cheery fire crackled in the hearth. The warm glow illuminated Adam's handsome profile, which was bent over a large, leather-bound tome in his lap.

I closed the double doors behind me. He looked up and gave me the smile I'd missed like a lost limb during my travels. "There you are."

I ran toward him and threw myself in his lap. The book slid to the floor, but we were too busy kissing to care. He tasted like home and I intended to make myself very comfortable there for a very long time. His hands came up to cup my face. His touch was warm and a tingle ran from my scalp to my toes.

When he finally came up for air, his gaze caressed my face. "Gods, I've missed you."

"Ditto, Mancy."

"How'd the meeting go?"

I shook my head. "No talk. Kiss." I dove back in for another round of tongue tango. Luckily he was willing to let me take the lead.

Before long, his hands snaked up under my shirt and cupped my breasts. I pressed into those warm hands and wiggled my ass on his lap. He pulled his lips just far enough away to say, "Keep that up and we'll put on a show." He nodded toward the open curtains on the floor-to-ceiling sash windows.

Normally, I wouldn't have cared, but with Giguhl's demonic rug rats running around at all hours, you couldn't be too careful. I sighed and put my forehead against his. "Then I think it's time to move this discussion upstairs."

He groaned. "Trust me that there's nothing I'd love more—"

"Do not say *but*."

"But," he began in an apologetic tone, "Giguhl's been pacing around the house all night asking when you were getting back. In fact, I'm surprised he hasn't busted in—"

At that exact moment, the doors to the library flew open. On the threshold stood a seven-foot-tall, scaly, green demon. He wore a red smoking jacket that complemented his black horns and hooves. Despite the distinguished attire, his expression was anything but composed.

"Bael's balls, Mancy! You promised to let me know the instant she got back."

I sighed and dismounted my man. "Hi, G."

"Thank the gods!"

"What's wrong?" I glanced at Adam, who

shook his head as if to say he took no responsibility for the demon. "Did you and Valva have another fight?"

Valva was Giguhl's wife. A marriage between a Mischief and Vanity demon already had enough built-in drama to fuel an entire season of reality TV shows, but when you added their litter of demon babies to the mix, it was downright combustible.

"Well, yeah," he said. "But that's not the issue."

"Did the kids destroy another car?" I asked.

His gaze skittered south. "Yes," he said in a quiet tone. "But we bought Brooks a new one."

My left eye twitched. "Giguhl, that's the third car they've eaten this year! You really need to set some boundaries."

"Hey! I'm doing the best I can, okay?" He threw open the lapels on his robe, exposing five distended teats.

"Jesus, Giguhl," Adam exclaimed.

"You try breastfeeding five demonlings when your teats are scabby and tell me how much energy you have for discipline!"

I closed my eyes and prayed to every goddess I'd ever met for patience. "We know you're doing your best. But please put your teats away."

I opened my eyes and was relieved to see he'd pulled the lapels closed.

"Okay, now take a deep breath and tell me what's got you all worked up."

He sucked a huge gulp of air and then exhaled it slowly. I nodded encouragingly, ignoring Adam's eye roll. He always said I gave the demon way too much leeway, but I had to keep reminding him that Giguhl wasn't officially my minion to order around anymore.

"Didn't you tell her?" Giguhl demanded of Adam.

I sighed, losing my patience. "Why don't you tell me?"

"Okay, so Erron's in town for the big concert on Halloween, right?"

I blinked. "Oh, that's right. And?"

"And he invited us over for dinner tonight."

The thought of going anywhere but to my bed was not a pleasant one. "I don't know, G. I'm pretty exhausted."

"You have no idea how hard it was to convince Valva to let me have a night off. We have to go!"

"Why don't you just go alone?"

The demon dug a hoof in the carpet. "Because…"

I raised my brows expectantly.

The demon finally sighed. "It's been so long since the three of us hung out together. I miss you guys."

My heart dropped. In truth, I had been so busy running the Dark Races I hadn't had much time for socializing at all. "Can't we just hang out here?" I offered.

He crossed his massive arms and scowled. "If we hang out here, the kids won't leave us alone and you'll just fall asleep."

I glanced at Adam, who shrugged, as if he hated to admit the demon was right. Exhaustion tugged at me like a gravitational force, but the hope in the demon's eyes was battering my conscience. "Okay, we'll go for an hour."

The demon let out a celebratory whoop.

"One hour!" I repeated. "Not a moment longer."

The demon waved a claw in the air. "Sure, sure. I'll go tell Valva," he called as he ran out the door.

I turned to Adam. "I'm going to regret this."

Adam rubbed my shoulders. "It'll be fun. Ziggy and Goldie will be there with the baby."

As much as I looked forward to seeing our old friends, his mention of the baby pinged my warning sensors. Ever since the demonlings were born, Adam had been dropping little comments here and there about the two of us jumping into the parenthood pool, too. I wasn't quite ready to swim in those treacherous waters, so I ignored the comment and focused on ensuring Adam helped enforce the only-stay-an-hour plan. "When we get home, I'm going to rip your clothes off with my teeth."

He turned toward the door and shouted, "Giguhl, let's hurry!"

∞

As a former resident of the Crescent City, Erron always came in a few days early for his local gigs and stayed a few days after. He even owned a home in the Garden District not far from ours. His visit this time coincided with Voodoo Fest, a large music festival that drew many of the biggest names in music to the Big Easy. Erron would be playing the main stage on Halloween with his band The Foreskins. Their first album, *The Devil's Bris*, hit all the charts, making them even more successful than his former band Necrospank 5000.

It was a brisk autumn night, so we headed out on foot since it was only about five blocks to Erron's house. Giguhl was with us, but he was in his cat form instead of his very conspicuous demon guise. Since it wasn't too cold I hadn't made him put on a kitty sweater. He'd argued with me before we left the house, but in the end, I'd told him he either let me do the spell to change his form or I wouldn't be going to Erron's at all. He'd relented and scowled at me during every second of the transformation from seven-foot-tall demon to hairless cat.

"Thank the gods," Giguhl breathed the minute the door closed behind us. "I was worried Valva wouldn't let me go."

Adam frowned. "Fatherhood getting to you?"

The cat snorted. "Nah, that part's fine. It's the

constant feedings."

I grimaced against the feel of his teats brushing my shoulders. "Why don't you wean them already?"

"Valva says we need to nurse them until they reach their maturity. She's determined to do everything the right way."

"Easy for her to say. They're not her teats." Demons didn't reach maturity until they were a millennium old.

"Sabina," Giguhl said in that tone parents get with nonparents. "You don't get it."

I adjusted my bra with my hand. "And I hope I never do."

A few minutes later, we walked up to the black iron gate that surrounded the house at the corner of Prytania Street and Third. The home had a fairly illustrious history of famous owners, but I always thought of it as Erron's orgy house. The first time I'd met the guy, Adam, Giguhl, and I had been staking out the house in an effort to find a murderous band of vampires we were hunting. But instead of vamps, we'd found Erron and his band hosting an orgy with a midget (who we later learned was named Goldie Schwartz), a gimp—in the S&M zippered leather mask sense—and a host of strippers who were snorting cocaine from the massive dining room table using hundred-dollar bills. A first meeting like that makes a lasting impression. Luckily, Erron had quickly proven himself to be a kick-ass mage and all-around stand-up guy in addition to his love of sex, drugs, and rock 'n' roll.

When we arrived, the house showed no signs of a wild party. In fact, the place looked downright charming with the French windows in the front glowing a warm welcome and the soft strains of classical music whispering from the front door. "Do we have the right place?" Adam asked.

I swatted him on the arm. "Behave."

Adam and Erron had an uneasy friendship. Erron was what the mage Hekate Council called a "Recreant," which meant he had shunned the council's laws. In Adam's opinion, this made Erron a loose cannon, but sometimes I wondered if the resentment had more to do with Adam feeling stifled by those same laws. Being the nephew of the leader of the Hekate Council came with a certain amount of responsibility, after all. Regardless, the two managed to get along most of the time.

I knocked on the door, and a couple of minutes later, a four-foot-tall woman (the stilettos added four inches) wearing a leopard-print pleather skirt, a black lace corset, and a ton of attitude opened the door. "The fuck you want?"

"What's shaking, Goldie?"

The scowl on her hot pink lips morphed into a grin. "Just my moneymaker, doll. Get your ass in here!"

She stepped back, opening the door enough to

allow all of us entrance. She hugged Adam's leg and took Giguhl from my shoulder to cradle him against her surprisingly ample bosom. The cat purred and nestled in like he'd found his favorite home. "Erron's in the kitchen," Goldie said, leaning in to nuzzle her nose to Giguhl's. "It's too bad we're both married, Gigi." The cat giggled, and I escaped as quickly as possible to be spared the flirtation.

Adam came with me, and we found Erron in the back of the house, where a huge modern kitchen had been built. The place was too pristine to have ever been the scene of actual cooking, but the attached bar had seen plenty of use. Case in point, Erron was pouring cocktails out of a shaker when we walked in.

"You made it!" He came forward to greet us. He wore faded blue jeans and a Bauhaus T-shirt, and his jet-black hair was expertly mussed. Several earrings sparked from both lobes, a chain with a pentagram hung around his neck, and a thick leather cuff wrapped around his wrist.

"Where's Giguhl?" he asked, pulling back from the hug he gave me.

"He and Goldie are making out in the foyer," Adam said. "Where's Ziggy?"

"He'll be down in a minute. He had to feed the baby." Ziggy and Goldie had had their first kid last year. It was hard to imagine two people so dedicated to the hard living of the rock 'n' roll lifestyle settling into parenthood, but they seemed to manage just fine. Erron had even had a special bus made for the family so they could bring the kid with them on tour.

Erron handed us our drinks and we held them up for a toast. "To the old times and the new times, but most of all, to the times we spend in the company of friends."

We all clinked glasses and sipped on the gin and tonics. Gin wasn't my usual choice of drink. I preferred vodka with extra blood, but I wasn't going to complain. Erron was right; it was nice to spend time in the company of friends. I'd spent so much time over the last year traveling that I missed the simple pleasures of being with the family I'd cobbled together. It had been a long, long road from being a lonely assassin for the Dominae to the leader of all the Dark Races, and I couldn't have gotten there without all of the beings in that room. Sometimes I got so busy I took them for granted—a habit I seriously needed to break.

"So you all set for the show?" I asked.

He shook his head. "I'm not sure it's even going to happen."

Adam and I exchanged a brief, worried glance. "Why?" I asked carefully.

"You remember, Rocco, our bassist?"

We both nodded. We'd met his entire band several times.

"Well, he did some scrying last week and seems to think that I'm going to die on Samhain."

This news was offered in such a casual tone that I didn't catch the meaning at first. But when it hit me, I took a nice, long pull of my drink to fortify myself. "Oh? Did he mention any particular mode of death?"

"This is serious, Sabina." The Recreant shot me an annoyed look. "Rocco's scrying mirror is never wrong."

"Please," Adam said, "we all know scrying is an imperfect arcane art. The symbols are open to almost any interpretation."

"He saw my heart stopping."

"Oh." Adam's mouth snapped shut and he shot me a look, inviting me to step in at any moment.

I sighed. "Is that all?"

He shook his head. "There were jack-o'-lanterns and a bunch of syringes lying around."

I frowned. "That's odd."

"No shit," he said. "I was really looking forward to that show."

Adam tilted his head. "And probably, you know, living."

He waved a hand. "A man doesn't live as hard as I have and expect to grow old."

Before we could question him further about it, Ziggy came down to join us. Fatherhood hadn't changed his affection for his trademark Rockabilly uniform. His arms were covered in tattoos that were hard to miss as his hands rose to use sign language to greet each of us. When I'd first met Ziggy, I'd been surprised to learn a deaf person could be a drummer, but as it turned out, he was able to feel the beat and rock harder than most.

After hugs were exchanged and more drinks were poured, we all headed to the dining room for the meal Erron had had delivered from Arnaud's. But before we could dig in, Brooks burst through the front door. Looking at his slight frame, bald head, and thick black glasses, it was hard to imagine that Brooks spent part of his time traipsing around in high heels, audacious dresses, and wigs. He wasn't in drag tonight, but he was definitely in full drama mode.

"Brooks?" Giguhl said. IHe was back in his demon form now that we were safely inside the house. And when the Changeling burst through the door, Giguhl had unfolded his impressive seven-foot frame from the chair and immediately went to greet his friend.

Brooks was all but panting when he spoke again. "Sorry I'm late, but there's some trouble at the club."

The Changeling owned a bar called Lagniappe in the French Quarter, which hosted drag shows a few times a week.

We all gathered around him to hear what was the matter. He pushed his shoulders back, ready to put on a performance. "Remember the new girl I told you about?"

Adam and I exchanged clueless looks. We'd

had no idea he'd hired someone new, but Giguhl nodded eagerly, clearly more in the loop. "The new waitress? Candy?"

Brooks nodded. "She didn't report in for work yesterday. I called and left a message but she didn't answer. So today, when I still hadn't heard from her and she didn't show up for another shift, I went to check her apartment." He took a deep breath. "Her roommate said she had a date two nights ago and hasn't been home since."

I frowned. Brooks had a love of drama, but he took his responsibility to his girls very seriously. "Any chance the date just went well and she's having too much fun to come home?"

Brooks grimaced. "Why not call her roommate so she won't worry?"

"He has a point," Adam said. "Any idea who the date was with?"

He shook his head. "Some vampire, according to the roommate. She said Candy seemed pretty excited about it."

Erron leaned back against a column in the foyer, sipping his drink. "You know anything about this girl?"

"She's a mage. Moved to town about a month ago from Los Angeles. She mentioned she was originally from New York, though."

I nodded. That made sense, since most mages were from the Empire State, as it was the seat of mage power in the United States. The fact Candy had lived in Los Angeles went a little way to explain why she might be into vampires, since the City of Angels was vampire turf.

"By the way she talked," Brooks continued, "sounded like she'd been bitten by the Big Apple instead of the other way around.

"Any idea what she did in L.A.?" Erron asked.

"She waitressed at a couple of bars."

"Have you called the police?" Adam asked.

Brooks's head shook so hard I was worried his glasses were about to fly off. "No cops."

"But—" Adam began.

The Changeling slashed a hand through the air.

"Why not?" I asked.

"Look, Candy was up front about some problems in her past." He then continued in a whisper. "Drugs."

Ziggy whistled and signed something for Erron to translate. "How do you know she hasn't just gone off on a bender?"

"That's what I'm worried about. If she has and we call in the cops, she'll go to jail."

Erron crossed his arms. "Sometimes that's what junkies need, Brooks." He said this gently, but it didn't soften the truth. Especially coming from the rock star who'd had his share of trouble with both drugs and the law in the past.

We all fell silent, waiting for Brooks's reaction. Finally, he scrubbed a hand over his scalp. "I won't do that to her. Not when we have enough resources in the room to find her." His eyes scanned the circle until they landed on me.

I started shaking my head and backing away before the words could even come out of his mouth.

"C'mon, Sabina. You're the leader of all the Dark Races. Surely you can pull some strings with the local vamps to see if they might know something about the vampire she went out with."

I grimaced. "That's the thing, Brooks. The local vamps and I aren't exactly on great terms."

Giguhl cleared his throat, the censure clear in the sound. I shot him an annoyed look. I really didn't want to get into the whys right then.

"Can't you call Nyx?" Brooks asked.

"I'm sorry, but I'm not bothering the leader of the country's vamps to see if she can find out who your friend had a date with."

Brooks glared at me. "This isn't like Candy. She's never even been five minutes late to a shift. My gut's telling me something's really wrong."

I softened my features and tried to look sympathetic. "I know you're worried about her, but there has to be another solution besides bothering Nyx."

"I could ask Rhea if she knows anything about this girl," Adam said. Rhea was his aunt, and she was also the head of the mage Hekate Council.

"That would be so great, Adam," Brooks said. I frowned at the exaggerated gratitude in his tone because it was clearly a passive-aggressive shot at me.

"Sure. What's her last name?"

"McShane," Brooks said.

Adam blinked and went pale. "Wait…is her real name Cadence?"

Brooks nodded. "How did you know?"

I tilted my head. "Wait…isn't that…?"

Adam swallowed and nodded. "Yeah," he said in a tone as grave as a cemetery.

Giguhl's nose perked up like a bloodhound on a juicy scent. "What?"

I crossed my arms as pressure started to build in my chest. Adam paled and backed away a step. "I, uh, used to date her."

"When?" Brooks asked, looking as intrigued as Giguhl.

"A while ago," Adam said.

"How long is a while?" Erron asked, joining in with the interrogation.

Adam backed up another step. Out of striking distance. "About three years ago."

Giguhl's mouth dropped open. "That's right before you met Sabina!"

Adam eyed the door. "I sort of broke up with her right before I met Sabina in L.A." Lucky for him, he'd already told me about his relationship with Cadence McShane or he'd already be knocked out on the floor. Still, knowing the history didn't erase my instinctive jealousy at hearing Adam talk about a woman he loved.

"How long before?" Brooks asked.

The mage shot the changeling a you're-not-helping glare. "Like a week. That's why I volunteered for the mission to find Sabina. Cadence went a little…nuts when I broke it off."

"How serious was it?" Erron asked. "Women don't usually go nuts unless they feel screwed over."

Those green eyes measured the distance to the door again.

"Adam?" Giguhl prompted, tapping his hoof.

He blew out a breath, as if surrendering to impending doom. "We were engaged."

The room fell silent as all eyes turned to gauge my reaction. "Relax, I already knew about it."

Audible sighs of relief filtered through the room, as if they'd expected me to murder the mancy any second.

"In that case," Brooks said, "does this mean you'll call Nyx after all?"

I frowned at him. "Why?"

Giguhl made a disgusted sound. "Adam's ex-fiancée is missing. The girl he screwed over to be with you, I might add. You have to help find her now."

"He didn't screw her over to be with me. They broke up before he even met me," I said, my voice holding a hint of warning. "But if Adam wants to help, he's welcome to." The mage in question cringed, hearing the warning in my tone—the one that said his reaction to that statement would determine whether he would spend the rest of eternity sleeping on the sofa.

He touched my elbow. "May I speak to you?"

I knew if I agreed, he'd talk me into it. He'd remind me that I was a good person, not some petty shrew who let jealousy rule her actions. But the shock of finding out Brooks's waitress was the same woman Adam had planned to spend the rest of his life with before I came into the picture hadn't worn off. I wanted to wallow in it a little while. I shook my head at his request. "I'm feeling exhausted all of a sudden. I'm going home." Before he could respond, I turned to Erron. "Thanks for the drinks."

And with that, I used magic to flash out of the house before anyone could argue with me.

∞

About two seconds after I flashed into our bedroom, Adam followed. That was the sucky part about being in love with a mage. "I knew I should have gone somewhere else." I started to flash out again, but he grabbed my arm.

"Don't. We need to talk."

I shook my head. "We can talk about it tomorrow."

He crossed his arms and raised that infuriating eyebrow. "Now, Sabina."

The old me would have been yelling and pacing around the room. But the problem with growing up and gaining some self-awareness was being able to recognize when you were acting like a brat. "I know it's stupid."

He sighed and took my hand in his. "Not really."

I jerked my gaze toward his. "Really?"

"I've had to deal with one of your exes, too, remember?"

I wasn't eager to talk about how I'd almost ruined my chances with Adam before we really even got started by briefly reigniting an old flame with Slade Corbin. Time for a change of subject. "I just don't see why we have to be the ones to find her."

"Because our friend asked us."

My shoulders dropped. I knew he was right, but I was so exhausted I wasn't ready to think about jumping into the drama. His hand caressed mine in a soothing motion.

"I hate that this happened tonight." He moved closer, wrapping his arms around my waist. I stayed stiff but didn't fight him off. "You've been gone so long and I was looking forward to an enthusiastic homecoming celebration." His forehead tipped to touch mine.

"Don't," I said. "Don't try to seduce me into feeling better."

What I really meant was I didn't want any sort of gentle lovemaking. I knew it wasn't his fault Cadence McShane had reentered our lives, but the petty part of me wanted to punish him for daring to love someone before I came along.

I'd been quiet for so long, he mistook my lack of encouragement as rejection. He began to pull away, but I grabbed his lapels and pulled him in for a punishing kiss. Unlike our passionate joining of lips when I'd first arrived earlier, this was a clash of tongues and lips and teeth. Despite the nips of pain, it was no less arousing.

I pushed him back toward the bed. He didn't struggle. Smart of him. If he wanted my forgiveness, he was going to have to let me take the lead this time. I wasn't interested in timidly lying back while he worshipped my body. I wanted to brand him with my body. Remind him that he belonged to me and me alone.

He fell back onto the mattress. The hem of his shirt folded back, revealing the flat, muscled planes of his stomach and those twin hip indentations that just begged to be nipped with my fangs.

I ripped his shirt open with a flick of my wrists. His eyes widened but heat sizzled from the depths. It had been so long since I'd pressed my skin to his, felt his hardness against my soft parts. Part of me wanted to relent my plan to punish and just curl up on him like a cat for some heavy petting. But I steeled my spine and slowly began unbuttoning my shirt inch by agonizing inch.

I was going to make him beg for it before the night was over. When I pulled my shirt open, he whimpered at the sight. I stuck a finger between my lips and got it nice and wet before dragging a trail from my collarbone down to the waistband of my low-slung jeans. "Want to see more?"

He swallowed hard. "Oh yes."

"Too bad."

His lips pressed together. "I see how it is."

"Do you?" I flung off his boots and socks. Then I ran my hands slowly up the legs of his jeans. Under the thick denim I could feel the corded muscles of his shins and thighs. I'd felt those muscles flex over me more times than I could count. I'd opened my thighs over and over so he could thrust into me. Had he done that with her, too?

"Ow."

I pulled back, belatedly realizing my caress of his balls had gotten a little…pinchy. "Sorry," I lied.

He shifted uneasily. I patted him gently. "Sorry."

He visibly unclenched and settled back into the mattress. "I'd feel a lot better if you didn't have any pants on."

I smiled. "You first." With a couple of flicks, I had his fly unbuttoned and the zipper down. Soon, the denim slid down his legs to reveal the muscles I'd touched earlier. The deep V of his hips, the hard ridges of his quads, the crisp golden hair on his shins—hell, even his feet were sexy. No doubt about it, even after all these years, he still did it for me. No other man had ever held my attention long enough or so thoroughly. And I certainly never could have imagined that a man as solid and well adjusted as Adam Lazarus would choose me as his life partner.

"Tell me you love me." I hated the neediness in my tone. I hated that I still craved reassurance after all this time. I was a freaking demigoddess, but this man had the power to bring me to my knees. He could strip me totally bare and destroy me with a single word.

He sat upright and reached for my stiff fingers. "Look at me." I swallowed and complied, even though part of me couldn't handle the intimacy because I knew he'd see the insecurity. "Sabina Kane, you are the love of my life. No one else matters. No one else even came close to what I feel for you."

I looked away. The words were nice and I believed him, but I still felt like crap.

He pulled me down to sit next to him. "Listen, why don't you just let me handle this situation? I'll help Brooks and you don't even need to be around Cadence if we find her."

I shook my head immediately. "Absolutely not. I'm not a wimp."

"I know that more than anyone else on this planet." He smiled ruefully, no doubt recalling all of our adventures and battles. "So what's the problem?"

I fought saying the truth because I knew it made me sound like an idiot. But he knew me too well to get away with a white lie. Time to come clean. "What if you see her and suddenly all those feelings come back?"

"Ah," he said.

"Ah what?"

He turned toward me. It was kind of hard to focus on his face with that gorgeous display of masculinity so close I could touch it and taste it. "You know what we have isn't normal, right?"

I frowned. "What do you mean?"

"I know you never had a long-term relationship before you met me, so maybe you think this thing between us—this intensity—is normal. That all people in love feel it."

I nodded. "Don't they?"

He laughed. "Some people who love each other can't even stand to be in the same room for too long, much less sit within two feet of each other without wishing they could rip each other's clothes off."

My brows rose, realizing the need I felt was also shining in his eyes. "So you didn't feel that way with Cadence?"

He shook his head. "I loved her, but it was different. I didn't realize at the time that it wasn't an all-consuming love. More of a tenderness."

The idea of Adam being tender with anyone but me made me want to put my fist through a wall—or my fangs through a jugular.

He held up his hands. "I can't believe you're acting so jealous. After all we've been through?" His fingers found the ring on the middle finger of my right hand. The one he'd given me the night he'd asked me to be his soul mate. Not a proposal in the traditional sense, but a vow to spend our lives together nonetheless. My shoulders softened as I remembered that night in Tuscany when we'd whispered promises to each other, neither sure we'd survive the next day, much less the rest of eternity, together.

Who was I kidding? What Adam and I had was real. Real real. I may not have loved a lot of people in my life, but I knew us. Nothing under heaven or earth would rip me away from this man, not even death—I'd for damned sure find a way to haunt him. And I had every reason to believe he felt the same for me. "I'm sorry," I said finally.

He frowned. "For what?"

"Not giving you enough credit. It's just the thought of you with someone else makes me feel a little insane."

His hands cupped my cheeks. "Trust me—I know exactly how that feels." I cringed a little, remembering him having to deal with this—and worse—when the Slade issue had come up.

"All right," I said, "so we're both fools where the other is concerned."

"Exactly." That crooked smile that always drove me crazy appeared on his full lips. "Now where were we?"

I stepped between his legs and placed my hands on his shoulders. "Somewhere around here."

He leaned forward and kissed my stomach. His

hands came up to circle my wrists with a firm grip. He whispered against my skin, "Lose the pants."

And for the next several hours I complied to that and many other requests with relish.

OCTOBER 28

The next evening I stumbled downstairs to grab some coffee before setting out on the Cadence hunt. But when I got to the kitchen, I walked through the door and almost turned to walk right back out.

"Sabina!" Valva called from the massive table on the far side of the room. It wasn't the demon's presence that made me yearn for retreat, but the demon children surrounding her. Dinnertime for the five demonlings was a horror I wouldn't wish on my worst enemies. "Giguhl said you were back. Come tell me about your trip."

I sighed and continued into the room. Valva was…persistent. Better to get this over with now than face a tantrum. Vanity demons could be pretty touchy. "It was okay."

Because of the disturbing sounds coming from the table, I opted to busy myself with making a pot of coffee instead of joining them. Even though Giguhl had yet to wean the little bastards, they still required a steady diet of raw meat. Demon babies are born with predator's teeth, so chewing wasn't a problem. A side of beef was lying on the table while the kids dug in like a pride of lions going after a gazelle. Only less civilized.

"Aynis, stop biting your sister," Valva chided. Then she turned back toward me with the forced smile of a tired mom. Although, unlike most moms, she had golden skin and a peacock tail that twitched whenever one of her kids shrieked over a bit of gristle. "So what's your deal, anyway?"

I blinked and looked up from filling the coffee carafe with water. "What do you mean?"

"Giguhl said you wouldn't help find Brooks's friend because you got your panties in a twist on account of the girl being Adam's old flame," she said with her trademark tact.

"Did he now?" I counted each scoop of chicory coffee slowly, hoping it would help keep my temper in check.

"I don't blame you."

I frowned and looked up. "Really?"

She shrugged. "If I found out Giguhl had hidden some whore from his past, I would grill his 'nads over a pit of hot coals." Her golden lips split into a wide smile. "While they were still attached."

"Whore!" The smallest demon, a blue-skinned

imp named Gooch, mimicked over a mouthful of bloody meat.

Despite the overly graphic description and the kid's interjection, I maintained a straight face. "In this case, I knew about the girl. I just had a little trouble with the shock of finding out she was in town."

She continued as if I hadn't spoken. "Who knows why men do what they do? They're all savages, really." She reached over and picked up a juicy rib from the pile and began delicately gnawing at it. "Still," she hedged, "I hope you'll change your mind and help my sweet Sticky Buns. He's missed you."

My conscience pinged. "I've missed him, too."

She set down the bone and licked her golden fingers clean. "Just don't get him in any trouble." She looked up slowly. "Or you'll answer to me."

Suddenly I wasn't hungry anymore. Valva was the daughter of Asmodeus and Lilith, the King and Queen of Irkalla, so she had some serious muscle behind her threat. But I wasn't worried about retribution from those deities as much as I was concerned about her just making life at home a nightmare. Or maybe it wasn't the threat ruining my appetite, but the effects of watching the demon babies tear into the carcass. Either way, it was time to get out of that kitchen.

Just then, one of the demonlings toddled away from the table. She was covered in golden scales and bright green fur sprouted between the two black horns on her head. "Auntie Sabina," she cried. Her claws were covered in cow goo, but I didn't complain as she threw herself at my legs.

I patted her little head. "Hi, Lulu," I said, calling her by her nickname. I refused to call her the name her parents had given her.

"Now, now, Auntie Sabina has very important matters to attend to, like ignoring her friends and punishing her lover."

I glared at the Vanity demon. A sharp pain bloomed in my right calf. "Ouch!"

Lulu pulled back with a bloody smile.

"Labya!" Valva cried, rushing forward to grab the kid by her arm. "No bite!"

The child giggled and licked her black lips. "Aunty Sabina tastes like candy!"

Thoroughly creeped out, I all but ran out of the room to go find Adam and Giguhl so we could get this damned wild-goose chase over with.

∞

In the library, I found Adam on the phone and Giguhl typing away on the computer. The look Adam shot me when I walked in was a visceral reminder of the fun we'd had after our heart-to-heart the night before. I shot him a saucy smile in response and went to join Giguhl at the computer.

"What's shakin', G?"

He used his claws to type something into the computer. "I'm chatting with Brooks. He wants us to come meet him at Zen's shop. He says he's got something to show us."

I sighed. The last thing I wanted was to wade into the sea of humanity clogging Bourbon Street to get to Zen's shop. With the Halloween crowds already taking over the city, the place was going to be a madhouse. "Can't he just tell us what it is over the computer?"

Giguhl shook his head. "Nope. The roommate found Candy's diary. He thought it might help."

Before I could respond, Adam hung up the phone. "That was Rhea," he said. "She's been in touch with Cadence's family, but none of them have heard from her since she left New York." His shoulders dropped. Seeing the defeat in his expression made me feel like an ass. Here I was feeling selfish when he was the one grappling with guilt over leaving the girl. "Rhea did say the last time they knew of Cadence's whereabouts she was in Los Angeles, so chances are good Brooks's waitress really is her."

I went to him and put my arms around him and squeezed. "It's not your fault."

He shrugged. "Yeah, it kind of is. We had problems long before I met you, but I could have broken it off better."

I sighed. "Well, you can apologize to her once we find her."

Both males paused. "Does that mean you're

in?" Giguhl asked.

"I'm not totally heartless," I said, filling my tone with plenty of martyrdom. "I'm capable of putting my personal discomfort aside to help Adam's old…friend."

Adam shot me a smile that made me feel like I'd gotten a gold star at life. "Let's head out, then."

∞

Madame Zenobia's Voodoo Apothecary was housed in a two-story building in the middle of Bourbon Street. While many of the shops in that area were tourist holes, Zen's place was an actual working voodoo emporium run by a bona fide voodoo priestess. Sure, the store got its share of foot traffic from the curious looking to buy a voodoo doll to take home as a souvenir, but the store was the real deal.

Since Halloween was just a couple of nights away, the population of the French Quarter was higher than usual. Instead of flashing to the store and risk being seen materializing out of thin air, we drove. We had to park several blocks away and then walk through the Quarter, weaving our way through the sea of inebriated humanity. When I'd first come to New Orleans, this overwhelmingly vulnerable mass of humans was both a temptation and an annoyance. But now, being in the middle of all that energy put a little extra spring in my step. For a city so focused on the past and so intimate with death, New Orleans was very much alive.

Giguhl, on the other hand, wasn't so enchanted. "This sucks balls," he groused from my arms.

"Ixnay on the talking in publicay," Adam said.

The demon cat hissed in response. You'd figure he'd eventually get used to the fact that he simply couldn't be seen in public in his seven-foot-tall, green-scaled demon form. "Just think of it this way," I said, keeping my eyes forward, "if you couldn't change into the cat body, you'd never be able to leave the house."

"Humph." The pissy feline flexed his claws against the sensitive skin of my inner arm.

"Ass cat."

"Trampire."

"All right, you two," Adam sighed.

I pressed my lips together and sidestepped a drunk coed puking in the gutter outside of Larry Flynt's Hustler Club. I soldiered ahead, determined not to let the demon's bad mood or the specks of puke on my boots ruin my mood. I'd been traveling so much on council business that having a few days to hang out with the old gang in my new hometown felt a little bit like a vacation. Maybe it's twisted and selfish to look at hunting down a drug addicted mage who may or may not be in major trouble as a lark, but whatever. I never promised to be selfless. I'd only promised to help.

A few moments later, we arrived at Zen's shop. The double doors out front were wide open and a warm glow from inside invited passersby to duck in and explore. And there was plenty to see. Every inch of wall space was filled with masks and shelves full of colorful bottles and gourd rattles and crosses and skulls. The air smelled of dust and dried herbs and something dark and spicy I couldn't begin to identify. When we walked in, a little silver bell rang near the back of the store, where a curtain separated the selling floor from the offices in the back. To the right of that was a staircase that led to the sleeping quarters upstairs and Zen's workshop.

Zen came out from behind the curtain. When she saw us standing there, she whispered something to the girl behind the counter and walked over to join us. Her braided black hair was pulled back into a ponytail. She wore a long, loose gown covered in a batik print. On another woman the dress would have looked frumpy, but she managed to make it look both elegant and earthy. Her face was tense and she didn't waste breath with pleasantries. "Brooks is upstairs." Then she turned on her heel and made her way up the steps, expecting us to follow.

She led us to the second-floor workroom, where she made all of her tinctures, poultices, and gris-gris bags. Drying chicken feet hung alongside bundles of sage and other herbs dried from long lines attached to the ceiling. A long wooden table, glossy and dark with age, bisected the room. Brooks stood on the side opposite the door when we all filed in. In front of him was a thick, leather-bound book, which he closed when we entered. "Where y'at?" His tone lacked the jovial Southern charm it normally contained.

Giguhl leapt off my shoulder onto the table and went to his friend. "How you doing?" He plopped his furless butt right next to the diary. I noticed Zen's eyebrows rise, but she didn't protest the cat tainting her sacred workspace.

Brooks shrugged and pushed his thick black frames higher on his nose. "Worried."

"Is that Cadence's diary?" I asked, ready to get down to business.

"Yeah. I hate to invade her privacy, but it's all we have to go on."

"Did you find anything?" Giguhl prompted.

Brooks nodded. "She had several diaries in her apartment, going back years. This one covers the last four years."

Adam tensed beside me. A quick look in his direction and I realized he was staring at the book in question as if it were a snake. That's when it hit me that the same diary that could help us find her might also contain secrets about her and Adam that he might not want me to know.

Part of me, the side ruled by the demon of bad choices, wanted to grab it and flip back to the time when she and Adam were together. But my more practical angelic side reminded me that picking that particular scab would only lead to unnecessary pain. The old me would have told the angel to take a hike and tackle the Changeling for the diary, but the new me, the one who enjoyed happiness and peace in my life, grabbed her man's hand and squeezed. This was awkward for me, but it had to be hellish for Adam.

He squeezed back and forced a smile before releasing my hand. "So what did you find out?"

Brooks didn't quite meet Adam's gaze. A sure sign he'd read the pages my bad-choices-side wanted to read so much. "For the last couple of weeks, her entries have mentioned the same name repeatedly."

"Well?" Giguhl asked.

"Damascus White."

Oh shit, I thought. "Damascus White, as in the leader of the New Orleans vampire coven?"

Brooks nodded and held up the book. "The weird thing is that even though she's pretty detailed with her entries, whenever she mentions Damascus, she's very sketchy." He opened the diary and read from it. "This entry is dated a week ago. 'Damascus called again. He won't take no for an answer.'"

Adam and I exchanged a look. "Why would the leader of the vampire coven be asking out a mage?" I asked.

"You're assuming a lot," Zen said. "He could have been asking her anything."

I nodded. "True. But still, with his resources, it seems odd he'd resort to asking a mage for help."

"Have you met him?" Brooks asked.

I grimaced and shook my head. "Not formally."

"Wait," Giguhl said. "Does that have something to do with what you said last night about not being on good terms with NOLA's vamps?"

I hesitated before nodding.

Several pairs of judgey glances shot my direction. "What did you do?" Giguhl asked on a sigh.

"It's all because of that time we came here to look for Maisie." My grandmother, Lavinia, had kidnapped my twin sister, Maisie, and brought her to New Orleans a couple of years earlier. Adam, Giguhl, and I had spent a few weeks in the Big Easy looking for Granny Dearest and ended up having a huge battle in a cemetery that ended in her demise. Good riddance. "I guess Damascus took over as the leader after a lot of New Orleans's vampires got recruited by Lavinia and her goons. Apparently we killed several of his friends, though."

Several groans filtered through the room.

"And then when we moved to town permanently, I was so busy trying to get the Dark Races Council up and running that I neglected to set up a meeting with White and he took it as a deliberate snub."

Adam frowned at me. "How do you know all this if you've never met him?"

I shrugged. "Nyx told me. Apparently White went to her to lodge a complaint. She called to tell me about it, but I guess the harm had already been done because when I offered to meet with him, he refused."

"Yep, that sounds like Damascus," Zen said, nodding.

"Wait, you know him?" I asked.

"Of course. Not that it's anything to brag about. He's a real jackass."

One of my favorite things about Zen was she didn't mince words. Plus she was an excellent judge of character. I blew out a resigned breath. "Well, if we want to get to the bottom of this, we're going to have to talk to him. Do you think you could arrange a meeting?" I asked her.

She laughed. "Please. He would never accept an invitation from a human."

"Well," Brooks said, "we definitely need to talk to him. The last entry in Cadence's diary mentions that she finally agreed to meet with him." He looked up. "That was the night before she went missing."

Everyone looked at me expectantly. "Crap. All right. I'll talk to Nyx."

Brooks's face cleared. "Thank you so much, Sabina."

OCTOBER 29

Nyx agreed to meet me the next night at Muriel's, one of my favorite restaurants in the Quarter. Luckily, she'd decided to stick around town after the council meeting to enjoy the Halloween festivities.

The room the maître d' put us in held a single table and two walls covered in racks of wine. A third wall held a large window that looked down on Jackson Square and the inky expanse of the Mississippi at night. Down on the street below, revelers were dancing through the streets in costumes with plastic cups of Abita or hurricanes from Pat O'Brien's clasped in their hands.

Nyx looked up as I approached. "How do you think they'd react if they knew monsters like us actually exist?"

I frowned at her pensive tone. "They're all too drunk to care."

I took my seat next to her and ordered a drink

from the hovering fae waiter who'd shown me to the table. He was of slight build and had long hair pulled back into a neat queue; most humans wouldn't know he wasn't one of their kind. I only knew he was fae because of the telltale lavender scent rising off his pale skin. I was glad he wasn't a vamp who might report the details of our chat back to Damascus White.

"So," Nyx began, "how was the trip to Europe? I didn't get to ask during that clusterfuck of a council meeting."

I rolled my eyes at the memory of the drama between Queen Maeve and Mike Romulus. "Everything was fine. Just glad to be home for a while. How are things in L.A.?"

She sighed. "I've got some old-school vamps protesting the laws we just passed allowing our race to interbreed with the others."

"Nothing too violent, I hope."

She made a dismissive noise. "Nothing I can't handle. Slade is meeting with some of them this week to try and make them see sense."

I laughed. "If anyone can set them right…" I let that comment drift off. As close as Nyx and I were, the fact she had been with my father and was now sleeping with my ex was still a bit of an awkward topic. Don't get me wrong, I thought she and Slade were perfect for each other, but it was still kind of odd.

The waiter delivered our drinks and proceeded to share that night's specials. We both ordered—

two steaks, bloody. Once he was gone, Nyx leaned forward across the table.

"You going to tell me the real reason you asked for this dinner?" she asked. "Not that I don't enjoy your company, but you don't normally go for the girls' night."

I took a sip of my Sazerac. "I need a favor."

"Of course," she said immediately. "Anything."

"I need to set up a meeting with the head of the NOLA coven."

"Damascus White? Why?"

"One of Brooks's friends is missing and we have reason to believe she's been in contact with White recently."

She paused before answering. "You believe he's involved in her disappearance?"

This is where I had to be careful. Even though Nyx and I were good friends, outright accusing one of her own with foul play was not a smart move. "We have no reason to believe he's directly responsible. Just want to see if we can piece together a picture of her activities before she disappeared. Her diary indicated she had a meeting with him. We're hoping he might be able to shed light on what she was into."

"Okay," she said. "I can arrange it for whenever you prefer."

"Sooner the better," I said. "Thanks, Nyx."

She smiled but it didn't reach her eyes. "Just be prepared for him to refuse."

A thin vein of embarrassment wove its way into my voice. "I was kind of hoping you could do some gentle arm twisting if that turned out to be the case."

She laughed. "I see. Well, I can try, but I'm afraid it's not like the old days when your grandmother ran the race."

My grandmother, Lavinia, had been the Alpha female in the triumvirate of vampires who had controlled the race for centuries. She'd led through a combination of violence, cunning, and more violence. Now, the structure of the vampire government was much more democratic, which was a good thing, even if it was damned inconvenient sometimes.

"Just do what you can. I promise to tread lightly with him."

Nyx made a strangled noise that one might mistake for a chuckle. "Just be prepared. You may have to do some groveling."

"We'll see." I pushed down the annoyance that rose at the humor in her tone. Adam's ex had better really be in trouble and not just off on a lark or I was going to kick her ass when we found her.

"Regardless, I wish you luck. If you run into problems, let me know."

Nyx was no slouch when it came to leadership, but the idea I couldn't handle a vampire was a little insulting. I was the granddaughter of the former Alpha Domina of the entire race.

Granted, I'd killed her, but still. I'd learned a lot of tricks about bending people to my will from Lavinia Kane. And if that didn't work, I'd just use the charm I'd picked up from the mage side of the family.

I polished off my drink. The sooner we found Cadence, the sooner Adam and I could get her back out of our lives. I wasn't about to let Damascus White throw a wrench in that plan. "Oh, I'm pretty sure he'll be the one with the problems if he refuses to help me."

OCTOBER 30

As it turned out, the meeting with Damascus White was arranged fairly easily. Word came from Nyx the next day that White wanted to meet that evening at a bar frequented by the fanged and fabulous.

That's how I ended up walking into an Absinthe bar in the French Quarter at half-past midnight the night before Halloween. I would have brought Adam with me, but bringing a mage to a vampire meeting wasn't just foolish—it was dangerous. Even though there was peace among the races, some old-school vampires still saw mages as prey instead of allies.

The front of the bar was filled with late-night revelers who'd stumbled in off Bourbon Street to get their first taste of wormwood liqueur with its cloying anise flavor. The place was done up in ornate Belle Époque style with thick green silk curtains, gas lanterns along the wall, and vintage lithographs inspired by the work of Jules Chéret and Toulouse-Lautrec. Ornate armchairs and divans provided comfortable resting perches for customers to watch the bartenders conduct the ritual of dripping the bright green liqueur over sugar cubes and adding water from ornate funnels that looked like they belonged in an alchemist's lab.

I passed the bar with a wave to Jean-Paul, the vampire who ran the joint. He was a friend of my old pal Georgia's, who'd moved to Los Angeles to work for Nyx. He jerked his head toward the back to indicate Damascus was already waiting for me upstairs in the Dark Races–only section. The upstairs area was a large open space that led out to a veranda that hung over Bourbon Street. Booths lined the walls, and each could be sealed off from the rest of the room using black velvet curtains. It created an intimate atmosphere that invited the sharing of confidences. Whether Damascus White was in a sharing mood or not remained to be seen.

It didn't take a lot to guess which booth my host inhabited. Two red-headed goons flanked the seams of the only closed curtains in the row of otherwise empty booths. Seeing them, I sort of regretted not bringing an entourage of my own. Not that I felt I needed protection. But vampires were all about displays of power.

One of the vamps stepped up like he thought he'd intimidate me as a warning before I spoke to his leader. I shot a glare that promised painful, fiery death if he so much as breathed on me. He stepped back. Smart of him.

Without much ceremony, I threw open the curtain. Damascus White sat dead center in the back of the booth. The power position. His face betrayed no expression at my arrival. His hair was red, like all vampires, but so dark it was almost black. He was old. Real old. Not as old as some of the vamps I knew in Europe, but old for American vampires.

"Thank you for agreeing to meet with me," I said.

His eyes were gray and too shrewd for me to let my guard down. Those eyes had seen things and missed nothing. He wore a velvet blazer and dark denim jeans that hinted that Damascus, despite all his years, had kept up with the times. "Had Nyx not interceded on your behalf, I would not be here."

"Going through Nyx was merely a formality. If you'd refused, we'd be meeting under much less comfortable circumstances."

He chuckled. "Careful, or I'll show you why they called me the Butcher of Belfast before I came to the States."

I failed to hide my complete lack of awe over his ridiculous nickname. "I'm here about Cadence McShane."

He frowned, as if I'd finally managed to catch him off guard. "Who?"

I smiled tightly. "According to her diary, Cadence was on her way to meet you the night she disappeared."

"Oh," he said with a twitch of his lips. "Her."

"Yeah," I said. "Her. What happened?"

"Never showed." As he took a sip from a glass of blood, I eyed him for signs of lying, but a vampire that old didn't reach his age without knowing how to tell a lie well. "I assumed she'd changed her mind."

"What were you two meeting about?"

His eyes flicked to mine and the corner of his mouth lifted. "Let's not play coy. I had every intention of fucking her and drinking that sweet blood. Not necessarily in that order."

If he'd been trying to get a rise out of me, he failed. Vampires loved mage blood. It was the extra kick of magic. Up until recently, mating between the races was forbidden by all the Dark Races ruling bodies, but since those restrictions had been lifted, there was a lot of interracial hanky-panky going on. Vampires might not respect mages as equals, but that didn't stop them from wanting a piece of their magical action, so to speak. "And when she didn't show, you just let it go? According to her diary, you'd been quite persistent with your pursuit."

"I may be persistent, but I am not desperate. When she didn't show, I decided it was time to focus my affections elsewhere."

My brows rose. "You really expect me to

believe that as the leader of a powerful vampire coven you were cool with getting stood up by a mage?"

"You may believe whatever you wish. That won't change the truth. I assure you I am not wanting for blood nor sex partners."

That I didn't doubt. First, he was beyond handsome in that predatory way of many vampires. Second, he was old enough to be a master of seduction. Third, in his position he could just take what he wanted. The question is, did he take Cadence, and if so, why was he hiding her? Or was she even alive?

I pushed aside that thought because I didn't want it to be true. The idea of having to be the one to tell Adam that Cadence was dead was too horrible to contemplate.

Time to try another tact with Damascus. I leaned back and watched him for a few moments. "Where did you and Cadence meet?"

He glanced away and back so fast a lot of people wouldn't have seen it. But I did. "A party."

"Which party?"

He shrugged and shifted in his seat. "Don't recall."

I pinned a pitying expression on my face. "Old age affecting your memory?"

"I am invited to a lot of parties." His reluctance to share the name of his host told me there was gold in this lead. The person who threw the party may not be responsible for Cadence's disappearance, but he or she damn sure knew something Damascus was trying to hide.

"Listen, asshole, I have been extremely patient thus far. But I assure you that I have reached the bottom of that barrel. It's time to give me the answers I want."

He leaned forward. "Or what? You'll use your special magic on me?"

For an elder vampire like Damascus White, my mage blood meant I was automatically inferior. The fact I was the Chosen, selected by the mother of all the Dark Races to lead her children, didn't matter to this guy. I leaned forward too. With a flash of fangs, I smiled. "I don't need magic to make you bleed."

He smiled then. "Is that a threat?"

"It's a motherfucking promise."

He laughed. "That shit might work on the faeries and weres, but around here it's a declaration of war."

I sighed. "You'd really go to war over a mage? I wonder what your followers would say about that."

He paused.

"Just tell me who hosted the party and you can walk away with your pride intact." He opened his mouth with a sneer, but I held up a hand. "If you refuse, my first step will be to call Nyx and inform her that you need to be removed from your post as coven leader. My second will be to introduce you to my friend, the sun."

I could tell from the spark of fear in his eyes that he'd heard all about how I was able to walk around in the daylight.

"They call him the Reverend."

"Who does?"

"Everyone."

"Vamp?"

He shook his head. "Adamite."

I frowned so hard an ache formed between my brows. "What the hell are you doing going to human parties?"

"The Rev knows all about the Dark Races. We're his best clients."

"Clients?" I asked. "Wait—he's a dealer?"

Damascus nodded.

"Was Cadence there to score drugs?"

He shrugged. "She certainly seemed to be having a good time," he evaded. "So much so that she captured the attention of many appreciative eyes."

"Yours."

He nodded. "And the Rev's."

I nodded, understanding. "You think he might know where to find her?"

He shrugged. "I don't care."

"Where was the party?"

He opened his mouth to lie again. I took my time removing my gun from my jacket. I hadn't wanted this to escalate so fast, but he was seriously wearing on my nerves. "I'd advise you to answer the question."

His eyes narrowed, promising that this was yet another reason he'd keep on considering me his enemy. "Near the Garden District. Lee Circle, I think."

I lowered the gun and scooted out of the booth. "That wasn't so difficult, now, was it?" I stood over him, waiting for the reply.

His lip curled and he looked up at me with the same expression someone might use for a pile of shit. "You're a real bitch, Chosen."

"Damn straight." I smiled. "Bye now."

∞

I went straight from the bar to Zen's shop. Turned out Brooks had plenty to say about this Reverend guy. "I've seen him around the Quarter. Everyone knows he's bad news. Got a gang of vamp goons to watch his back."

I sat back in a chair in Zen's living room. "Damascus said he's a dealer."

Brooks's eyes darkened. "Kind of. He's more of a pimp, you ask me."

Zen frowned. "Prostitution?"

Brooks shook his head. "He hooks vampires up with drug addicts."

"Shit," I said. "Blood junkies are the worst."

Adam and Giguhl walked in then. I'd called them on the way over and asked them to join me so we could come up with a plan. Adam got one look at my face and obviously realized I had bad news.

"Tell me."

"She's taken up with a group of blood junkies."

Adam's face went pale. "Shit."

"Blood junky?" Giguhl asked.

"Vampires who gets off on drinking blood from drug addicts," I explained. "They get their blood and their drug fix in one."

"And since Cadence is a mage, they'd get a third high from her magic," Giguhl concluded.

"Where is she?" Adam demanded.

I told them what I knew about the house where Damascus had attended the party. Brooks nodded. "I think I know the place." Judging from his tone, we weren't headed to the Four Seasons.

"You guys stay here and I'll go check it out."

Adam cleared his throat and crossed his arms. "Like hell."

"It's not safe, Sabina," Brooks said. "Those vamps she's hanging with? They're ruthless."

I opened my mouth to respond, but Adam spoke up. He looked more pissed off than I'd seen him in a long time. "We'll show them ruthless."

∞

The old Victorian might have been impressive back in its heyday, but now it looked like something out of a creepy horror film. Three stories of rickety wooden bones with paint peeling like decayed skin. Half the windows sported holes and the others were completely missing. Beer bottles, cigarette butts, and stray animal feces littered the weedy front yard. This place hadn't just been abandoned. It'd been desecrated.

From my vantage point across the street, I could sense some movement inside. Giguhl sat on my shoulder in cat form. "What you picking up, G?" I asked.

He lifted his snoot and sniffed the air. "Besides body odor and the scent of despair? I'm picking up enough dirty copper smell to mean we're dealing with at least six vamps."

"How about you, Mancy? Getting anything?" Adam was on the roof of the house. He'd flashed up there shortly after we arrived. We'd borrowed walkie-talkies from Zen. Brooks was up there with him because he'd claimed, as Cadence's friend, he should be allowed to help.

"Quiet up here."

"Don't go in until G and I are in position."

"Yes, ma'am," he said. I could tell by the tone of his voice he was looking forward to this as much as me. With all the worry and speculation, it was nice to be doing something active. The chance to kick some blood-junky ass felt like a play date in the middle of a shit storm.

"Okay, here's the deal. I'm going to try this the

polite way first," I said. Giguhl snorted. Ignoring him, I continued. "If they don't cooperate, we go with Plan B."

"Which is?" Adam said through the speaker.

"Crack some skulls."

"Sounds like my kind of plan."

With that, Giguhl and I made our way across the street. It was late by mortal standards, nearing two in the morning. But I could see dim lights from near the back of the house. As we neared the rickety front steps, I could also hear the occasional bark of laughter or the impact of glass shattering. A radio somewhere deep inside the structure played grating music—the kind preferred by people whose senses were so numbed out by drugs they needed to be overwhelmed to feel anything.

Giguhl shifted on my shoulder, his claws digging into my clavicles. "I have a bad feeling about this joint, Red."

"Drug dens are rarely happy places, G." I rapped my knuckles on the door, putting a little English on it so it would be heard over the racket of the music. After a few moments of pounding, the door flew open.

I stepped back as the odor of urine, vomit, and unwashed bodies blasted me in the face. The vampire who stood before me looked like Iggy Pop, only with faded red hair. The bad hair life wasn't due to needing a salon visit. Instead, the effect of the drugs he was getting from the humans he fed from was leeching all the color from his body. If he'd been human, it would have sucked all the life from him, too, but I wasn't really sure that was worse than an eternity of addiction.

"What the fuck do you want?" he demanded. His lips were ashy and chapped, and his fangs were gray.

"Hi there," I said in my most chipper voice. "The Reverend around?"

He squinted at me, noting the cat on my shoulder. "You the fuzz?"

I tilted my head and smiled. "Any policeman you know walk around with a bald cat?"

He sucked on his rotten teeth. "I thought I might be seein' things."

"Understandable." I waved a hand. "But no. I'm not a cop. The Rev?"

"He ain't here." He started to slam the door, but I caught it.

With a tight smile, I held the door open. "Then maybe you know my friend Cadence? She's about yay big." I mimed a height slightly shorter than mine. "With brown hair and blue eyes."

He smacked his pale lips in disgust before yelling over his shoulder. "Yo, is there a Cadence here?"

A faint voice carried down the stairs. Female. Cadence? I'd never met her, so I didn't recognize the voice, but then I could barely even make out the words. But apparently the drugs hadn't hurt Iggy's hearing.

"Who wants to know?" he echoed the shouted question.

"Sabina," I said with patience.

Iggy screamed my name up the stairs. A few seconds later, he cocked his head to listen. Then, with a resolute nod, he slammed the door in my face.

"Well, that's that, then," I said. I spoke into the walkie-talkie. "We're a go. In three...two..."

Bam! I kicked in the door with my heel. Luckily I'd traded my stiletto boots for the more practical, low-heeled variety or the move might have broken my ankle.

I expected a flurry of reaction—bodies flying, screams, the usual. Instead, Giguhl and I barreled into the foyer and found it totally empty. With my gun drawn, I rushed toward the back of the house. Here and there, vampires lay on the floor like blinking, languid cats in pools of sunshine. Only it was nighttime, the pools were yellow but definitely not caused by the sun, and something stronger than catnip had those dudes tweaking.

I'd often wondered why vampire drug addicts didn't cut out the middle man and just insert the drug of choice directly into their own veins or lungs or whatever. But I guess something about the narcotics mixed with blood made the effects stronger. Regardless, a vampire junky is just about as uncomfortable to be around as a human one, only vampire junkies have the added bonus of predatory instincts, superhuman strength, and immortality to go along with their need for speed, as it were.

When no one so much as gasped at our entrance, I figured we were safe heading upstairs to try and meet up with Adam and Brooks. None of these lazy sons-a-bitches was capable of a rear attack.

"Put me down, Red," Giguhl whispered.

"Trust me when I tell you, you do not want your bare paws touching these floors." Each step I took was accompanied by a wet sucking sound as my soles struggled to free themselves of the sticky human stew covering the rotten wooden planks. "Just hold tight and keep your eye peeled for Cadence."

When we reached the top of the steps, Adam was just reaching the same level, only from the attic. He looked around, eyes wide. "Remind me to shower in rubbing alcohol when we get back."

"I'll get your back for you," Brooks said, patting the mage's shoulder.

Adam rolled his eyes but a smile flirted with the corners of his mouth. "Let's split up. You guys take the two rooms at the front of the house. Brooks and I will get the rear."

I nodded and took off toward the first room I came across—a bedroom, filled with filthy bodies. In the corner, two lumps grunted under a ratty blanket. Junkies needed love, too, I guess.

With a sigh, I realized that, just like downstairs, the inhabitants were a mix of human and vampire—no mage in sight.

"Cadence?" Giguhl whisper-yelled. I thought about correcting him. After all, he was usually under strict orders to keep his trap shut in cat form. But I would bet cash money this was not the first time many of these people had witnessed a talking, hairless demon cat. The only difference was this one wasn't a figment of their scrambled minds.

A groan made my ears perk up. Over in the corner, I saw a flash of dirty brown hair—instead of vampire red—as a person rolled over. Was that a random vampire moving in her sleep or Cadence trying to stay hidden? No choice but to wade through and see.

I tiptoed through the garden of junkies, picking my way gingerly lest I step on a hand or a foot or a needle still attached to a vein. Finally, I was close enough to see my target in the corner. Nope, not Cadence. Not even female, as it turned out. Although, to my credit, it was pretty hard to tell. Everywhere I looked, there were bodies emaciated to the point of androgyny.

"Do you see her?" Giguhl whispered.

I shook my head. "Let's try the other room."

I expected more of the same in the next room. However, when I opened the door, I realized I'd stumbled onto the main feeding room. While the areas I'd witnessed so far seemed to be the lounging spaces, this place was where the real action happened. Iggy was there, sitting in the corner, feeding off a teenaged boy—probably a runaway. If the rude vamp noticed us, he didn't show it. Instead, his eyes rolled back in his head, showing nothing but the whites as the drugs from the teen's blood hit his own bloodstream.

I dismissed that pitiful scene because something far more interesting demanded my attention. A female vampire bent over a female's neck and eagerly slurped at the bloody wound. "Cadence?" I said carefully.

The female vamp's head jerked up. Her fangs and chin were covered in red and her eyes were dilated full black. The girl between her legs looked up more slowly, but the instant those two hopeless blue eyes met mine, I knew we'd found our girl.

"Cadence." Louder now. Not a request for attention. A demand.

Unlike the other inhabitants of the house, Cadence looked relatively healthy. Her skin wasn't covered in scabs and her body hadn't begun to waste away into a heroin skeleton. But her arms were covered in alternating needle tracks and fang marks. And those eyes were too haunted.

"I told you to leave," Iggy said from across the room.

"I know." I kept my eyes on Cadence. "I'm not a very good listener."

Slowly, the vampire straddling Cadence pulled back. She didn't bother to wipe the blood from her face.

She flashed her gray fangs and growled, "No one wants you here."

I speared the junkie with a glare that would have made a sober being think twice about crossing me. With casual slowness, I raised my gun and pointed it between her black-hole eyes. "Get the fuck out of here before I deliver something even more toxic than smack to your system."

She laughed, the sound not unlike an ass's bray. "You stupid bitch. Bullets won't hurt me." She spread her arms wide, as if daring me to shoot her.

"You're right. The bullets won't hurt you until the apple cider embedded in their core takes effect."

Her eyes widened. Apples were vampire Kryptonite. It went back to the origins of our race in the Garden of Eden, and Eve's apple, which robbed humans of their mortality. Since Lilith, the mother of our race, had already fled the garden by then, she'd remained immortal. As her children, vampires were also immortal—unless their blood was exposed to the forbidden fruit.

The vampiress shot a worried glance at Iggy. His face morphed into a pained expression. Apparently this was all too taxing for his system.

The vampiress grew bored waiting for his reply

and clapped her hands together. Sparks flashed between her fingers. "I'll zap you before the bullet leaves the barrel." She'd been drinking mage blood, which meant she could do rudimentary magic. But she couldn't control the power enough to be a real threat, and besides, I was a motherfucking Chthonic demigoddess.

Before I could inform her of this fact, a throat cleared. I turned to see Adam standing behind us. "If you don't leave right now, that bullet will be the least of your fucking problems." He raised his hands. An arc of bright blue power flashed from his fingers to hit a chandelier overhead. The next instant the light fixture crashed down in a spray of crystal and metal not a foot from where the vamp-bitch stood.

After that, she was nothing but a blur of red as she fled past us. Iggy followed, hot on her tail.

I hoped she would wise up enough to just remain scarce until we left, but as tweaked as she was, she'd probably shamble back with reinforcements.

Adam rushed across the room, where a shell-shocked Cadence remained on the floor. If the altercation with the vampire had scared her, she didn't show it. In fact, when Adam reached for her, she scrambled away, albeit sluggishly. "Don't touch me!"

"Cadence, it's me—Adam."

"I know who you are," she hissed. "Get out! I have nothing to say to you."

"I have plenty to say. Later. In the meantime, we're leaving."

"Not me," she said. Her tone was languorous and thick. "But you're welcome to go."

A gasp sounded from the doorway. I rounded and saw Brooks try to rush in just before Adam restrained him.

"Candy!" Tears ran down Brooks's face. "What are you doing to yourself? Listen to Adam. It's time to leave, baby girl."

She licked her lips and shot Adam an angry glance. "I can't believe you brought Brooks here."

"I can't believe you brought yourself here. What the fuck, Cadence?"

Cadence pulled herself into a standing position with unsteady movements. "Take your judgment and get the fuck out, Adam."

See, this was where things were going to get hairy. No one, but no one, talked to my male that way. Especially not junky ex-girlfriends we'd risked our necks to save. My first instinct was to forcibly remove her from the house, but given her anger and the drugs skewing her judgment, chances were good one or the both of us would get seriously injured. I tensed with indecision but quickly received a nudge from the demon cat on my shoulder.

"Let him handle it," the cat hissed in a low tone.

"I know you're angry," I said in a calm voice. "But you're not punishing anyone but yourself."

Her eyes snapped toward me. "Who the fuck are you?"

My mouth fell open. I shouldn't have been surprised she didn't know me, but I was. Before I could tell her, Adam stepped between us, blocking me from her sight. "Don't worry about her right now."

My eyes narrowed.

"Let me take you out of here," he said in his most persuasive tone. Then he whispered things I couldn't hear.

I clenched my fists and tried to remind myself he was just trying to get her to agree. Still, it wasn't easy to watch.

"It hurts, Adam." Her voice wobbled. "I just don't want to hurt anymore."

He nodded and took a cautious step forward. "I know it does." When she didn't balk at his advance, he took a couple more steps. "But I'm here because I care about you. Let me help you."

"You can't help me." Her words were thick, like her tongue had swollen to twice its normal size. "No one can." She swayed on her feet.

Adam rushed forward to grab her. She tried to fight off his assistance but stumbled into his arms instead. I stood nearby feeling helpless. She thought drugs could erase her pain, but she was wrong. Only time and getting real with yourself could heal emotional wounds.

Cadence sobbed into Adam's chest. He patted her back and murmured soothing words, but his gaze was on me. He raised his brows to ask what our next move was.

"What the fuck is going on in here?" a male voice boomed from the doorway.

I turned slowly to see a man standing in the doorway with a small army of vampire tweakers behind him. He wore the collar of a holy man, but the long bleached hair, blue jeans, and crocodile boots ruined the pious look of the ensemble.

"The Reverend, I presume," said Giguhl from my shoulder.

"That or someone's dressed up for a Halloween party," Brooks said.

"Which is it, mister?" I tilted my head. "That a shitty costume or are you really the Reverend?"

If hearing a cat talk shocked the human, he didn't show it. He tossed his long hair and sneered. "Who the fuck's askin'?"

"Who we are is less important than why we're here," I said.

Behind me, I felt magic rising on the air as Adam prepared for a showdown. I hoped it wouldn't come to that, but I was also prepared to cut through those junkies like a needle through a vein.

"Well?" the Rev asked.

"We've come to get our friend."

The Reverend's eyes narrowed. "By whose authority?"

I pulled my gun out and pointed it at him.

"Smith and Wesson's."

He laughed and removed a gun from the hollowed-out Bible in his hands. "They're gonna have to take it up with my old friend Mr. Glock."

I sighed. "Look, asshole, you've got a lot of junkies there, but I've got two mages, a Changeling, and a demon with me."

"And what are you?" he said, sounding unimpressed to be facing down a bunch of dark race badasses. "Some kind of mixed-blood?" He spat the term out with enough venom to tell me he was acquainted with dark race politics. Mixed-bloods were the lowest of the low up until the leaders revoked the law forbidding interracial mating. Unfortunately, he wasn't as well versed as he thought if he didn't realize who I was.

I smiled. "My name is Sabina Kane—maybe you've heard of me?" He didn't look impressed, but I wasn't done. "And all you need to know about me is I have an itchy trigger finger."

"And if I were you, I'd be worried about the call I made to Damascus White just after I was alerted to your intrusion."

The sounds of screeching brakes sounded from out front.

I frowned at him. "You work for Damascus White?"

The Rev shook his head. "We're business partners."

"Ah," I said, "he gives you protection in exchange for a cut of the blood money you get for pimping addicts to vamps?"

The Reverend smiled in a way that reminded me more of the Devil than a man of the cloth. "Yes, ma'am."

If Damascus White really was behind the Reverend's operation, he'd likely arrive with a lot of goons, like those he'd had with him the other night. Which meant things were about to get really fangy and unpleasant.

"Why would Damascus White tell Sabina about this place if he's the one behind the operation?" Adam said.

"Probably assumed the girl would be dead and dumped before you got here."

"Why would he assume that?" Adam demanded, his voice edged with acid.

The Rev shrugged. "Because he called me right after your meeting and asked me to kill her before you came snooping around." He frowned at me. "Which would have worked if you hadn't moved so fast."

Anger boiled in my midsection. I'd known Damascus White was dirty, but he'd managed to fool me into believing he wasn't involved. "Sorry to fuck up your plan, but we're taking her with us."

"Sabina, we should go," Brooks said, his voice high with panic. The Changeling was more a lover than a fighter.

"Not just yet," I said. "I'd like a few words with Mr. White first."

I started to step toward the door, but Adam's voice rang out like a shot. "Stand down, Red. We're leaving. You can deal with Damascus later."

"Bullshit." I rounded on him. "They can't just—"

Adam's gaze was hot as he stared me down. "We can't risk it. She needs help now!" He glanced down at Cadence, who was passed out in his arms. A rivulet of blood dripped down her throat.

Before I could answer, several things happened at once. Giguhl shouted something, and at the same time, a loud bang split the air. Searing heat exploded in my shoulder. I looked down to see blood blooming under my white tank top.

"Ouch! Godsdammit!" I shouted. "This is my favorite shirt."

The Reverend's expression morphed from satisfied to terrified. "But…but why aren't you dead? That was an apple cider bullet."

I smiled wide enough to flaunt my fangs. "I'm a demigoddess, dumbass." I marched forward and grabbed the gun from his hand. "Fuck!"

The good news was I was fine, except for the searing pain to both my shoulder and my pride. The bad news was, the gunshot spurred Damascus and his goons to speed up their entry. The front door crashed open, quickly followed by the sounds of boots on stairs. "We've got to go,

Red!" Adam yelled.

I realized then that if we tried to fight our way out of the drug den, we'd all be leaving with more holes than we entered with. No, walking out wasn't an option. That left—

"Circle up!" I coldcocked the Reverend in the face with the butt of his own gun. His eyes rolled back in his head and he collapsed in a heap. Behind him, the junkies slunk away like rats deserting a sinking ship.

I adjusted Giguhl on my shoulder and moved in at the same time Damascus appeared in the doorway. His gaze hit mine like a punch. My hand itched to challenge the son of a bitch. But my instinct to fight was overridden by the stronger desire to ensure the safety of the beings I cared about. "Hold on, everyone!"

Just as Damascus ran toward our small group, the vortex rose and we disappeared. His voice followed us into the void. "This isn't over!"

He was right about that much, but his comeuppance would have to wait until Cadence was stable. Dammit.

∞

When we got back to Zen's shop, we materialized in her sitting room. The voodooienne was elsewhere, so I sent Giguhl off to find her. Meanwhile, Adam carried Cadence's weight to the sofa. She was in and out of consciousness. I preferred her passed out because consciousness brought with it angry sobs that wracked her whole body.

While Brooks knelt next to Cadence and covered her with a blanket, I pulled Adam aside.

He blew out a long breath. "Gods, she's in bad shape."

"No shit," I said. "Let's hope Zen's got the patience to get her through the detox."

He frowned at me. "She's a mage. It shouldn't take as long to get the junk out of her system."

I sighed. "It won't take long, but it's more extreme than what humans go through because of the speed."

As if on cue, Cadence started retching. Brooks yelped and leapt back. Thinking quickly, I grabbed a nearby trash can and swooped it under her face just in time for the projectile vomiting to begin. The mixture was a pungent slurry of puke and black bile.

It was at that moment that Zen and Giguhl ran into the room. "What the hell?" the voodoo priestess demanded.

"Her body's ridding itself of the drugs," I said, trying to avoid the splash zone.

Giguhl cringed back. "It smells like Satan's taint!"

Zen disappeared into the kitchen off the salon and soon the sound of running water reached us over the noise of Cadence's heaves.

Brooks whimpered and moved restlessly from

foot to foot, clearly not sure how to help. Over her shoulder Zen said, "Brooks, go get the ginger root from my workroom."

The Changeling hesitated. But Zen shot Giguhl a look that communicated it was his job to get the faery out of the way. "C'mon," the demon cat said. "I'll help you."

Reluctantly, the faery picked up the cat and the pair exited. I moved closer now that the area around the couch had cleared out. "Ginger root isn't going to help with this nausea."

The priestess rubbed Cadence's back and nodded absently. "Yeah, I don't have any in the workroom anyway."

"Then why—" I stopped myself, realizing she'd just been trying to get rid of the audience. "Actually, why don't Adam and I go see if we can help them, too?"

Zen shot me a grateful look. "Thanks, Sabina."

With one last look at Cadence's pale, sweat-covered face, I grabbed Adam's arm and pushed him out the door. Zen might have thought I was just trying to give Cadence some privacy, but honestly, I was having some trouble being in the room. The smell alone was bad enough, but worse was seeing Cadence so weak and pitiful. It's not that I didn't feel bad for her, but being around that kind of vulnerability always made me edgy.

OCTOBER 31
HALLOWEEN

On Halloween afternoon, the news ran a story about how the old Breaux mansion on Lee Circle mysteriously burned to the ground overnight. When the anchors began speculating about the cause, I turned off the TV and went to join Giguhl on the couch. He was back in his demon form since we were in Zen's private living quarters. So when he looked at me, his black lips and goat-pupil eyes flashed a worried expression.

"Was it him?" He nodded to the door.

I nodded but didn't say anything. Adam had left just before sunrise claiming he needed some time alone. He'd returned a couple hours earlier without a word and resumed his vigil by Cadence's side.

On the one hand I totally got it. The things going down in that house were downright evil. It couldn't have been easy to see the woman he once wanted to spend his life with being used by vampires looking for a fix. But on the other hand—well, I'm not proud of the other hand. That hand was wondering if seeing her in that situation had woken up some latent feelings for his former love. The kind that made him commit wildly romantic gestures.

He's never burned down a crack den for me, I thought.

"Don't be an idiot," Giguhl said.

I paused. I knew I hadn't said anything out loud. "What?"

"I can tell your brain is going places it best not go. That Mancy loves you more than anything in this world. Don't let jealousy make you do some stupid thing."

I crossed my arms. "I'm not an idiot."

"Sure you are."

"Thanks, G."

He nudged me with his shoulder. "Sabina, we're all idiots when it comes to love. Trust me, if one of Valva's exes showed up, you would see me do some epically ridiculous shit. And if that happened, I would also hope you could smack me around a little and remind me to get a grip."

I pressed my lips together. "Maybe you're right."

"Um, hello? I'm wise as shit. You should totally listen to me all the time."

I shot him a look.

He frowned. "Most of the time, anyway."

I nodded. "Sometimes you do drop some epic

truths on my ass."

"Damn straight."

I sighed. "Okay, so I won't go all psycho girlfriend here, but I still feel like shit."

"Understandable," my best friend said. "But you shouldn't take that out on Adam. You should take it out on Damascus White."

I smiled, appreciating him trying to point out the positives. "Thanks for trying to cheer me up, but I'm afraid that honor will fall to Nyx since she appointed him." I'd called her the minute we'd gotten Cadence stable. She'd insisted I stay out of it to keep the peace among the races. Since he worked for her, it was up to her to deliver punishment.

"Maybe she'll let us help torture him a little," he said, still sounding hopeful.

I sighed. "A girl can dream. It's been a long time since I got to kick some serious ass."

What I didn't say was that part of me was relieved not to have to deal with Damascus. For once it was nice to let someone else deal with a clusterfuck. I still wanted Damascus to pay for what he'd done to Cadence and gods only knew how many other innocent people, but I trusted Nyx to deliver swift and potent retribution.

My cell phone rang and the screen told me it was Queen Maeve calling. I groaned out loud. I considered ignoring it, but I'd basically threatened her to give me an answer on the were issue before Samhain or I'd crack some metaphorical skulls.

"Hey, Maeve."

She made a squeaky noise to indicate her displeasure over my informal address. "Sabina," she said in a sour tone, "I have Michael Romulus conferenced in."

"Sabina," the werewolf said in his deep voice.

"Does the fact that you're both calling mean you've reached an agreement?"

"Yes," Maeve said. Michael made an assenting tone to support her answer.

My shoulders lowered from beneath my ears. I hadn't realized until that moment how much I longed for good news. "That's great."

"There's just one little addendum," Michael continued in a more hesitant tone. "We'll need your approval to move forward with it."

My high hopes began to plummet. "What is it?"

"I will only sign the treaty if there's a section added forbidding mating between fae and weres in my territory," Maeve stated in an imperious tone.

My mouth fell open. "Maeve, that flies in the face of all the progress we've made in tearing down those old walls."

"As it happens, I agree with her," Michael cut in. "Our race has struggled too long to keep our population strong and pure to begin diluting it with weak fae blood."

Maeve made an annoyed sound and added, "And my court has maintained its purity for millennia. It would be a shame to taint it with such primitive genes."

I sighed. "And if I refuse to allow the addendum?"

"Then I will refuse to allow the migration of any and all were packs into my lands."

My shoulders fell. As much as I wanted to promote a more accepting attitude among the Dark Races for mixed-bloods, it took a long time to change thinking on such ingrained attitudes. "I'm not happy with this at all. Changing the rules again so soon might encourage rebellion, especially among the younger members of your races." I sighed and bit the bullet. "But if this is the only way to reach a peaceful conclusion to negotiations, I'll allow it."

"Really?" Maeve said, her tone shocked.

"You didn't think I'd agree?"

"Not really." She sounded deflated, as if this addendum had been a ploy to make me refuse the agreement.

"Have your people write up the documents and we'll sign them at next month's session. I just hope this won't come back to bite both of you in the ass." After that, I got off the phone fast before I ranted at both of them and rescinded my approval. Sometimes dealing with dark race leaders was more frustrating than corralling Giguhl's kids.

Just then, Adam opened the door from inside the workroom. He scrubbed a hand through his hair, but he didn't look as hopeless as he had earlier. "She's awake."

We all stood and I went to Adam. I gave him a hug, and the minute his arms came around me and I sniffed his sandalwood scent, I knew I'd been an idiot. This man was mine and I was his. "How are *you*?"

"I've been less shitty, but I'll live."

"Can we go see her?" Brooks said from the doorway. I guess he'd heard us talking from down the hall.

Adam nodded. "She was asking for you."

Brooks didn't need any further prompting. He practically ran across the room. Giguhl followed closely behind. Adam and I followed more slowly. When I crossed the threshold, I couldn't see around Giguhl's massive shoulders. Zen's voice rose above the crowd, reminding everyone to take it easy because Cadence had been through a lot. A quieter female voice responded to Brooks in whispers.

I pushed past Giguhl and pulled up next to Brooks. Cadence broke off and looked up at me. Her eyes were wide and I could tell she was nervous. But she looked fifty times better than she had when we pulled her out of that house. Her hair was long and brown with gold highlights. Her eyes were a bright, clear blue and her complexion was getting some glow back. The only sign of her ordeal were the large bandages on her wrists and throat.

As much as I hated to admit it, I totally saw what attracted Adam to her. She had a classic, unthreatening beauty that a lot of men went for. But I also saw the shadows in her eyes. The ones that hinted at deep pain in her life. Of hard lessons and a lack of love. I recognized those shadows because I had them, too.

I glanced back at Adam. Maybe he was attracted to troubled women, I realized with a jolt. But I pushed that thought aside. Everyone has shadows. It's just, well, some of us have a harder time of disguising them. Turning back to the girl in the bed, I tried to smile.

"Hi," Cadence said.

I waved lamely. "Hey."

"You're Sabina, right?" Her eyes flicked behind me, toward where Adam stood close to my back.

I nodded and swallowed. Why was I nervous? "I'm glad you're all right," I mumbled for lack of anything brilliant to say.

The corner of her mouth lifted like I'd made a joke. "Thank you." The gratitude was offered so easily and genuinely that I couldn't continue to hold on to the negative feelings toward her I'd been trying to cling to. "Adam's told me all about you. I'm"—she heaved a shaky sigh—"I'm glad he's happy. You've been good for him."

I frowned. It never occurred to me that they'd be talking about me in the room all that time. I shot my Mancy a smile. "He's been good for me, too." I turned back to Cadence. "And I'm glad you're all right. You had all of us worried."

Her gaze hit the floor. "I know you won't believe me, but I wasn't using. At least, not before the Rev took me."

"What happened that night?" Brooks said, his voice careful.

She swallowed hard. "Damascus had been after me to meet him for a date. But when I got there, the Reverend was waiting instead. He tried to get me to go with him, but when I refused he—" She cut off and shuddered. Brooks patted her hand. "He shot me full of smack."

She paused, as if trying to collect her thoughts. "Next thing I remember is waking up in that house. They kept me so drugged I didn't even know how many days had passed before you guys arrived." She began to shake uncontrollably. "Thank the gods you found me. I was so—" She shook her head and started crying.

My heart sank for her. I had no idea how she'd recover from the wounds she'd suffered in that hellhole. But looking around the room, I thought maybe Cadence had more friends than she realized.

A throat cleared behind me. I turned to see Erron in the doorway. He wore huge, dark sunglasses that hinted at a bender the night before. "You're still alive!" I teased, referring to the prediction his bassist had made about his heart stopping.

"So far, so good." A line formed between his brows. "Weird, though, because Rocco is usually dead on with his predictions."

Giguhl came to join us by the door. He and Erron high-fived. "Isn't your show tonight?"

"I just came from the sound check. Brooks called to say you found your friend, so I wanted to stop in."

I nodded and turned to motion toward Cadence. Before I could say anything, though, Erron froze. I looked from him toward where Cadence lay in the bed. Her tear-stained face was a mask of shock, too.

"Um…?" I said.

Erron jerked out of stillness with a gasp and his hand went to his chest. "Ow."

"Dude, are you okay?" Giguhl whispered.

At that point, Brooks, Zen, and Adam had all clued in that something was going down. While Zen rushed to Erron to check on him, I kept my eyes on Cadence. She didn't look worried about Erron's health. Instead, she tilted her head and met his gaze across the room. The clouds behind her eyes cleared and a small, mysterious smile tilted up the corner of her mouth. "Oh," she whispered, "it's you."

Erron pushed Zen and Giguhl away with a muttered, "I'm fine." He took a couple of steps toward Cadence, his hand still on his heart. "Do I know you?" he asked.

She shook her head. "I'm Cadence."

"Erron," he said dumbly.

That's when I realized what was going on. Erron's bandmate hadn't seen the singer's death. He'd seen that Erron was going to meet a special someone who made his heart stop.

Cadence held out her hand, as if it were the most natural and normal thing in the world to reach for a man you'd only just met. While the rest of us looked on, flabbergasted, Erron walked directly toward her, took her hands in his, and leaned over to kiss them. "I think—" he began, and cut off.

Cadence smiled, the expression making her look younger. "Don't think," she said. "Sit."

With a look I can only describe as shell-shocked, Erron Zorn, lead singer of The Foreskins, Recreant mage, and all-around bad boy dropped onto the bed and gazed at Cadence McShane like she was his own personal goddess.

The room fell awkwardly silent for a few beats before Zen took control. "All right, everyone. Let's give her a chance to rest."

Giguhl, Brooks, and Adam filed out as instructed, each looking more confused than the last. I turned to go just as Erron started to stand.

"No," Cadence said, "you're staying."

Zen covered her smile with a hand and came to guide me out the door. Just before the panel closed, I saw a look of such uncomplicated connection pass between them that my eyes got a little misty.

When I turned away from the door, I found the hallway empty. I passed the living area and saw Brooks, Zen, and Giguhl chatting away and making a meal. "Where's Adam?" I asked.

Giguhl shrugged. "Said he needed some fresh air."

I paused and glanced toward the stairs. Adam had been through a lot in the last twenty-four hours. First, having to see Cadence in that drug den and then helping her through the horrible detox. And after all that, witnessing her and Erron Zorn fall under each other's spell like that.

Talk about an ass-kick of a night.

I found him leaning against a lamppost just in front of the store on Bourbon Street. The crowd was thick as the annual Halloween parades crawled through the French Quarter. Beads and candy flew through the air, and every sense was assaulted by color and light and music and screams and the scent of spilled beer and the turned-soil-and-blood scent of humanity. Normally, I would have enjoyed the sensory overload, but that night it felt…too much.

On one side of Adam was a man in a werewolf costume; a woman in faery wings stood on the other. I nudged Tinkerbell aside and put my arms around Adam. "You okay?" I whispered.

His arms came around me, and instead of answering, he kissed me with a passion that robbed me of breath and left me dizzy. When he finally pulled away, he was smiling. I blew out a breath. "What was that for?"

He put his forehead against mine. "I was just remembering the first time I saw you."

I laughed. "In that bar in Los Angeles."

He nodded. "I fell in love with you at that moment."

I shook my head at him. "While you watched me kill that guy?"

He kissed me again, too quickly for my liking. "No. The second you strutted in looking for a fight. I thought, 'There she is.' And you know what?"

"What?" I whispered.

"I was right. The minute I saw you, there was never a chance I'd ever settle for another woman." He glanced back toward Zen's building. "If I had to guess, that's exactly what Erron just felt in there."

I chose my words carefully. "So you're not upset?"

"About Erron and Cadence?" He chuckled. "Hell no. I'm relieved. I've felt guilty for a long time about breaking things off with her." I must have betrayed some emotion on my face because he caught my hand and squeezed. "Guilt isn't the same thing as regretting it being over. We didn't belong together. I just hated to know she was hurting. But now?" He took a deep breath. "I think she has a lot of work to do to get her life on track, but it's headed in the right direction."

I smiled at him. "You're a good male, Mancy."

He leaned forward and pressed a quick kiss to my lips. "I'm best when I'm with you."

Now my eyes really did sting with tears. Maybe it was the exhaustion or the emotional stress, or maybe it was simply relief of being reminded that what we had was as real as I'd hoped it was. To dispel the tears, I glanced around at the celebrations surrounding us on all sides. After a couple of seconds, I realized something. "You know, it was on another Halloween that we finally admitted our feelings for each other."

He smiled the same smile that had made me fall for him. "That year was the best trick-or-treat ever."

I raised a brow. "How are we going to top it this year?"

With a wicked smile, he caught a handful of beads and candy from the air. "Depends on what you're willing to do to earn these." His expression took on a particularly roguish tilt.

And with that, Adam and I flashed out from the middle of the parade, for once not caring who witnessed our magical exit.

What started out as a crappy week had turned out to be one of the best Halloweens ever. A night when the lines between monsters and men were nonexistent. A night when the most hopeless beings could find a light in the darkest shadows. And it for damn sure was a night to believe that sometimes even monsters deserved happy endings.

About Fire Water

Magic is a drug.

In this *Prospero's War* series prequel novella, rookie cop Kate Prospero only has one more training assignment to pass before she's officially sworn in to Babylon Police Department. But the veteran cop in charge of the river patrol boat is a salty old guy isn't happy about playing tour guide to a rookie and seems even less interested in real police work. But while on patrol, they stumble on to what appears to be a floating dirty magic lab. This highly combustible situation might finally be the key to these two unlikely partners finding common ground.

Fire Water

Pretty much any cop can tell you the story of their first arrest. Also the first time they pointed a gun at someone—or had one shoved in their face. The first handcuffing, the first black eye, the first time a perp puked on them—and, for some, the first person they killed.

My first collar wasn't all that memorable. Just a speeding ticket that led to an arrest for outstanding warrants.

My second was mildly more interesting, but not exactly earth shattering. Underage girl selling three-dollar blow jobs in an alley off Stark Street. When she'd seen me coming, she hadn't fought at all. Not surprising since I basically caught her with a mouthful of incriminating evidence.

No, my first two busts weren't that impressive. Sure, the second got a couple of laughs when told over beers at O'Malley's near the Cauldron cop shop. But it wasn't a contender for best war story compared with some of the fucked-up shit the veteran cops on our squad had seen. Working in a magical ghetto didn't have a lot of advantages—except when it came to outdoing your cronies with fish tales of junkie wizards and potion-peddling homunculi.

However, my third bust was the stuff of Cauldron legend. Ever since it happened, cops in Babylon referred to it in hushed tones and begged me to retell it over beers. But to me, it was more than just my go-to war story.

It was the story of how I became a real cop.

My name is Kate Prospero, and I bust magic junkies for a living. Most girls don't grow up dreaming of chasing perps through dark alleys and cleaning puke out of their squad cars at the end of an average night of work. I didn't, either. In fact, when I was eight, I told my fourth-grade teacher I wanted to grow up to be just like my uncle Abe. Miss Cope's eyes had grown really wide and she backed away like she was afraid to say the wrong thing and risk Abe finding out.

The dream of becoming the next Grand Wizard of the Votary Coven had lasted only until I was seventeen. And then I didn't have any dreams for a long time because I was too busy trying to survive.

But that was a long time ago. Now I'm on the right side of the law. It pays a lot less than potion cooking, but it beats spending your life with one ear constantly listening for sirens.

So anyway—my third arrest…

It started on a hot August afternoon five years

ago. I was still a rookie, and per the Babylon Police Department policy I was making my rounds through each of the major departments shadowing veteran officers. Apparently it hadn't always been that way. Used to be, rookies were sent straight out to patrol with a badge, a gun, and a walkie-talkie. But after too many newbies ended up potioned in the gutters, someone in the commissioner's office wised up that maybe the academy wasn't doing a good enough job training people for the rigors of patrolling a magical ghetto.

Anyway, I'd already made rounds through the vehicular theft department, the murder squad, the sex crimes unit, and even done a few ride-outs with deep night Arcane patrols. I'd seen lots of action, but hadn't been allowed to get in the middle since I was both an untested cop and an Adept. Mostly those assignments involved lots of coffee runs and hazing. But I'd learned plenty watching cops who'd seen it all do their jobs. The only department I had left to shadow was the river patrol division.

According to the other rookies who'd already completed their time on the boats that patrolled the Steel River, it was by far the most boring assignment. It's not that there's no crime on the water surrounding Babylon. The news was always filled with news of caches of alchemical materials confiscated from freighters out of Canada. The problem was, the Coast Guard always got credit for those busts. Mostly the BPD was in charge of the river and only provided backup to the Coast Guard on the Lake Erie cases.

I knew all this the morning that I pulled my Jeep into the parking lot near the docks. Even in the early-morning sun, the river didn't glisten or sparkle like most bodies of water might. If you kind of squinted, you could see past all the trash and the thick algal slime that collected along the banks. But nothing could disguise the stench of gasoline, chemicals, and rotten animal carcasses wafting up so strong from the water, you could swear the odor had a vaguely pukey color. Years of serving as the highway for barges bearing slag and asphalt from factories had ensured the water didn't flow so much as it oozed.

The police boat creaked at the gray dock. The vessel was white with red lettering announcing it as a Babylon Police Department watercraft. There was a covered portion with sirens on top along with a smattering of antennas. This wasn't one of those fancy Coast Guard vessels, since it mainly patrolled the river and not the Great Lake with its tides and heavy currents. Still, the boat looked watertight and maintained to my uneducated eye. Even though I'd grown up in Babylon, I spent as little time on or near the water as possible. I'd avoided the river for obvious reasons, and the lake because I didn't trust any water that I couldn't see through. Which was why I'd resisted the water patrol assignment until the very last week of my training. Well, that and Cap'n's reputation was well known, even among the recruits.

I grabbed my gear and jumped out of my Jeep, Sybil, with more gusto than I actually felt. Since I was practically right out of the academy, I was still fueled by the enthusiasm of the recently converted. I still bought into the belief that I could make a real difference and that justice would always prevail. I was also young enough to believe that my background on the street combined with my cop training meant I could handle just about anything the world threw at me.

In other words, I was naive as hell. So with an idiot's zeal, I tossed my holster over my shoulder, gripped my duffel bag in my right hand, and marched down the dock toward the boat.

"Hello?" I called.

The creaking of the boat and the slap of the water against the hull were the only responses. Frowning, I grabbed one of the wooden columns on the dock for balance and stepped into the boat. The instant my second foot hit the deck, a quiet, ominous male voice spoke from inside. "Ask for permission to come aboard."

I squinted into the darkness of the pilothouse. "Sorry?"

"You sure are," the gruff voice grumbled. A large silhouette moved forward in the shadows until the light outside caught a head of white hair and a face that looked like it knew its share of gin and smoky bars. "You should always ask before you board a man's vessel."

I blinked a couple of times. "Are you Captain Smiley?"

His chin dipped. "I'm still waiting."

I sighed and adjusted the gear weighing me down. "May I please come aboard?"

"Cap'n," he offered.

My eye twitched. "May I please come aboard, Cap'n?"

"Well now, that depends."

"On what?"

"Your business."

I looked pointedly down at my police uniform that clearly showed my name badge. Surely someone had informed him that I'd be coming. Just in case, I removed the orders from my pocket and waved the white sheet in front of me like a truce flag. "I'm Officer Prospero? I'm supposed to shadow you for the next week."

His right eye squinted, giving him a decidedly Popeye-esque appearance. "Fucking rookies."

And with that he confirmed about every rumor I'd heard about the infamous Captain Martin Smiley. Word was he'd gotten stuck on water patrol because he didn't get along with anyone. Not just other officers, either—anyone, period.

"Keep your paper," he snapped. "I already told them I wasn't playing babysitter."

I pursed my lips to keep from mouthing off to a superior, even if said superior was a Grade A jackhole. "Sir, no offense here but I'm just trying to finish off my hours. I don't want any problems."

"Me, either, which is why I think you should get off my boat and go find another asshole to annoy."

In order to get promoted to patrol, I had to get through this week with high marks on the reference forms or be forced to repeat the exercise until I passed. Most of the other rookies from my graduating class had chosen to do their hours on the more exciting Lake Erie patrol units, but since most of those time slots were at night, I had to skip them. I couldn't afford a babysitter to watch my brother all night until I was making full-time patrol pay instead of the part-time pay I was earning as an officer-in-training. So the daytime river patrol slot was my only option.

I took a deep breath and called on my training in dealing with difficult suspects. "Captain Smiley, I'm sorry you're frustrated. Perhaps we could just both calm down and talk about this rationally."

He waved a hand and continued raveling a long rope onto the deck of the boat.

I gritted my teeth. "Maybe I should call your commanding officer, then," I called.

A salty cackle was the only response.

I crossed my arms and tried to regroup. If a threat to call his boss didn't worry him, then it probably wasn't a great idea. After all, how many captains or lieutenants wanted to get a tattletale phone call from a rookie?

"Can I just ride along? I promise I won't get in your way." I figured if I showed up and watched him work it might count as shadowing. I could worry about talking him into signing my forms later.

He threw down the end of the rope and rose to his full height. "You're a real pain the ass, aren't ya?"

"Yes, sir."

He sighed. "All right. But you're gonna sit your ass still and not talk. One peep and I'll dump you into the drink."

I drew a deep breath into my nose. Instead of inner peace, the move only earned me a snootful of the stench of decayed fish and algae. Once again, I started to step onto the deck. He raised a brow and watched me with a sharp look. I paused, realizing he'd been testing me. "Does that mean I have permission to come aboard?"

He sighed, as if faced with a hopeless case. "Get your ass on here already."

This was going to be the longest week in history.

∞

That evening I had an appointment before I went to pick up Danny from his summer day camp. Now that I was about to start earning a full cop's salary, I could finally move us out of the one-bedroom apartment we'd been living in while I put myself through the academy. The rental house was in a better area of town, which also happened to be closer to Meadowlake, the private school I wanted to transfer him to in the fall.

The ad in the paper claimed the house had two bedrooms, two bathrooms, and a large backyard. Sounded perfect, but I'd been disappointed before. Even if the place wasn't a shithole and the rent was reasonable, there was still the issue of dealing with asshole landlords. The guy who'd owned the last place I tried to rent had denied my application because he "didn't want any dirty Sinisters ruining his property."

Even though I'd been running into prejudices about being an Adept my whole life, it still stung. Especially when I'd had to explain to Danny that we couldn't move into the house with the great swing set after all. When he'd asked why, I lied and told him someone else got there first. He'd already had so much bullshit to deal with in his short ten-year life, I didn't have the heart to tell him some asshole thought he was tainted because he'd been born a Lefty.

When I pulled up in front of the house, I was instantly charmed. The place wasn't large, but it was obviously taken care of by the owner. Trimmed shrubs on either side of the front steps and a maintained yard added a dose of charm to the bungalow-style architecture. Fresh black paint on the railings and the shutters on the windows.

A cheerful wreath on the front door. It was certainly nicer than the apartment we'd been living in, and the neighborhood was close to the school and mainly made up of senior citizens and young families. Yep, I thought, I could definitely do this.

I climbed the steps to the front door and knocked on the screen. A faint voice called out that someone was coming, but I stood out there for a good two minutes before I heard the sound of the dead bolt unlocking. A moment later the door opened to reveal a woman with long gray hair wearing a housecoat, which was made from blue fabric covered in pictures of cat faces. She leaned on a cane, and her skin was as wrinkled and thin as rice paper. "Yeah?"

"Hi, I'm Kate. I called about renting the house. Is Mr. Tanner here?"

The woman sucked her teeth and looked me over for a moment. "Tanner couldn't make it. Asked me to show you around."

"And you are?"

"Baba." That's all she said, as if I was supposed to recognize the name the same way one might Madonna or Cher. "I live over there." She jerked her pointy chin to the right, toward the house next door. Unlike the porch we stood on, which was surrounded by carefully trimmed hedges and neat little clusters of flowers, hers was surrounded by neatly trimmed rosemary bushes. Clumps of green and purple lavender dotted the walkway.

"So…may I look around?"

The old woman narrowed her eyes. "Depends."

"On what?"

"Do you listen to loud music?"

I frowned. "No."

"Do you throw wild parties?"

I shook my head.

"What do you do for a living?"

Her interrogation was quickly losing its charm. "I'm a cop."

Whatever she'd been expecting me to say, that wasn't it. "Like on *The Blue Devils*?" Her tone held a hint of excitement.

"The TV show?" I shook my head. "I'm afraid it's a lot less exciting than they make it out to be on TV."

Her face fell. "Oh." For some reason I felt like I'd failed some sort of test. "Come on in, I guess."

She shuffled back to allow me entrance. I stepped inside, surprised to find myself in a kitchen. A window over the sink shared the wall with the door and looked out onto the front yard. Along the wall perpendicular to that was the stove and next to it the refrigerator, which looked like it had been around during the Carter administration.

In the center, a square table was surrounded by four metal chairs with seats covered in apple-green vinyl. The linoleum underneath was worn but clean. "There's two bedrooms up and another room in the walk-out basement that could be a bedroom or storage room. Laundry's down there, too."

She took me through a short hall off the kitchen, which led to a bathroom and a bedroom. Aged hardwoods covered the floors in the bedroom, and a large window let in streams of cheerful sunshine. A painted iron bed was covered in a multicolored quilt. It was light-years away from my normal style, but I was instantly charmed. "Does the furniture come with the place?"

She shrugged. "You'd have to ask Tanner, but I assume it's negotiable."

I nodded. "Can I see the rest?"

She flicked her arthritic fingers toward the door. "Suit yourself. I'll be in the kitchen if you have any questions."

I walked back out and continued into the den. There a denim-colored couch and plaid armchair were both angled toward a small TV on a stand that wasn't made from wooden boards and cinder blocks like the one in my current apartment. I turned to see Baba in the doorway.

"Isn't it odd for the front door to be in the kitchen?"

She crossed her arms. "The front door used to be there"—she jerked her thumb toward the side wall of the den—"but the previous owner wanted more space. So they turned the side door into the front." She shrugged. "Worked out since the house is on the corner."

Where the front door used to be, there was now a dining room table. I didn't host any dinner parties, so I figured it would make a good place for the kid to do homework. I paused, realizing it was a good sign if I was already picturing our lives in the house.

I checked out the bedroom on the other side of the main floor. It was small but perfectly fine for a ten-year-old boy. Back through the den, I found a set of stairs leading down to the basement. Unlike most houses, there wasn't a door separating the living area from the basement. Baba explained this was because the downstairs had been converted to be part of the living space of the house.

Downstairs, the laundry room turned out to be just a hallway with a washer and dryer shoved under a couple of narrow windows set high into the wall.

A door separated what Baba had called the third bedroom from the rest of the basement. The bedroom was larger than the ones upstairs. A built-in desk lined one wall and a twin bed was shoved into the opposite corner. There weren't any windows to add light to the space, so a row of track lights hung from the ceiling. One door led to a tiny bathroom, which was extremely basic but serviceable. Another door led not to the closet I was expecting, but to a large storage room. At present the only things stored in there were dust bunnies, but it was large enough that I could cancel my rental on the room at the Store-A-Lot, which would save me about a sixty bucks a month.

The back door was next to the laundry space. The walk-out basement setup was due to the fact that the house was situated on a slope, but just outside the door the yard leveled off. A couple of steps down led to a patio area, and beyond that a dilapidated garage hinted that there used to be a driveway. I went to the garage and pushed the door open. The sudden sound of flapping wings greeted my arrival. When no other critters came running out of the darkness, I stepped inside.

It took a moment for my eyes to adjust to the dimness, so my other senses kicked on. The air was cooler in there, like a cave. The air smelled of old gasoline, paint thinner, and wood shavings. It was a comforting, solid perfume. It spoke of Sundays spent doing yard work while Danny played in the tree instead of listening to the freakhead neighbors having another fight.

My eyes finally adjusted enough to see a workbench set against one wall. A row of solid wooden shelves stacked above the work surface. Someone had lined up rows of jam jars containing screws and nails and other items commonly used in do-it-yourself projects. It was a space dedicated to fixing things, and I loved it instantly.

A shadow filled the open doorway. I turned to see Baba huffing from the exertion of descending the basement steps. "Well? What do you think?"

I took in a deep breath of the garage's perfume and smiled. "I'll take it." I moved forward to shake her hand. In my excitement I held out my left hand instead of my right.

Baba froze and looked down at my extended hand. "Hold on—you're a Lefty?"

I jerked my hand back. Stupid, stupid, stupid, I thought. No use lying now. "I am." I put my chin up and dared the old woman to make an issue of it.

"Tanner don't much like Lefties."

"And you?"

Her face crinkled into a smile that made her wrinkles dance. "I'm a witch."

I groaned inwardly. I hadn't known many human witches in my life, but my few experiences hadn't been great. While Adepts got all the credit for being able to wield magic, there were some Mundanes capable of harnessing magical energy, as well. Granted, they were incapable of harnessing as much power as an Adept and their power was strongest in groups, but it was there nonetheless. Mostly Wiccans and solitary witch practitioners specialized in hedge or kitchen magic—basic herbs and rituals using everyday items. Their magic wasn't categorized as either dirty or clean as an Adept's might be, but there was some movement in certain communities to regulate Mundane magic the way Adept magic had been.

"Oh," Baba said when I took too long to answer, "you're one of those."

I frowned. "One of what?"

She pointed at me. "One of them Adepts who think Mundane magic users are posers."

"Don't be ridiculous."

She raised a white brow. "Hmmph."

"Look, I would really appreciate it if you don't mention to Mr. Tanner that I'm an Adept. I promise I'm just looking for a safe, clean place where I can raise my little brother. We aren't troublemakers."

She shot me a skeptical glance. "I dunno. I'm not sure I want a bigot next door."

I raised my hands. "Give me a break. You have no idea how much discrimination I've had to deal with, lady. The last two places I tried to rent denied me because of being an Adept."

"You sure that's why? Not because you throw wild sex parties?"

I held up my hand in a fake scout's-honor gesture. "I haven't even had sex in three years."

Her mouth fell open. "Jesus, Mary, and Jerome, girl! That's no way to live."

I shot her a bemused look. "No shit."

She laughed out loud.

"So—" I drew out the word. "—does this mean you'll help me with Tanner?"

She blew out a breath and shot me what she probably thought was an intimidating look. "I need to think about it. Had a newlywed couple come by just this morning."

My hopes dipped. "Well, I'd appreciate any help you could give us, ma'am."

"And don't call me ma'am, either. Everyone around here calls me Baba. Got it?"

I fought my smile. "Got it."

∞

The next morning Cap'n was in an even worse mood. "Ugh, you again."

"Good morning."

"Thought you'd give up after yesterday."

I'd kept to my promise and not said a word the entire four-hour ride the day before. Mostly the patrol consisted of him listening to baseball stats on the radio while he made laps up and down the river. A couple of times, he'd stopped to warn someone going too fast in a no-wake zone or untangle trash from a buoy. Not exactly the exciting life I'd imagined when I'd signed up to become a cop. Still, I kind of found myself enjoying the breeze through my hair and the slower pace despite the constant stench of pollution and the dying wildlife.

"I'm just trying to do my job."

"Hmmph," he said. "Well? Come on."

The water under the boat boiled as he turned

on the engine. I hopped on board and headed toward my designated seat.

"Go grab that line, will ya?" The request was so unexpected I froze. "You ain't deaf, are ya?"

I shook my head and hopped toward the railing. The line he'd mentioned was the rope tying the boat to the dock. I basically knew nothing about boating, but I was pretty sure him asking me to help with anything counted as a victory. For the time being, Cap'n had decided to tolerate my presence on his vessel.

I unwrapped the line and was careful to coil it into a neat pile like I'd seen him do the day before. Once it was done, I turned to give him a thumbs-up. He shook his head at my enthusiasm and turned to pull the boat from the dock.

It was another sunny day. After the harsh Babylon winter, the sunshine and warm temperatures felt like a miracle. I even spied a few sunflowers peeking out from the piles of trash lining the shore long the lake. I smiled and chose to see them as a sign that my life would be in full bloom soon, too. I just prayed I'd hear soon about the house.

"Sit," Cap'n ordered.

I took a seat without a word. The boat chugged along the river for a few moments before I realized we'd gone a different direction than the day before. "Where we headed?"

My seat was actually a bucket shoved just outside the cover provided by the boat's wheelhouse. The position allowed me to enjoy the sun on my face, but also gave me a view of Cap'n's profile. When I spoke, his lip curled like he'd just smelled something rotten.

"Thought I told you not to talk."

I rolled my eyes. Surely he didn't expect me to stay quiet the entire week. I crossed my arms and turned toward the rail. If he wasn't going to tell me where he was going, I'd just try to learn by watching.

We were headed upriver, away from Lake Erie. Eventually the river would fork off into two branches, but for now it was a single, wide, polluted channel. As if to prove my point, a large hunk of wood floated past carrying a rat as large as a dog eating a bloated fish. I shook my head. At some point, something really needed to be done about the river. Everyone in Babylon knew that the rule was that if you fell into the Steel River, you went straight to the emergency room. Over the years the steel industry and lack of regulation had turned it into a dumping ground of chemicals, petroleum, and trash. Every now and then, you'd see a large bubble of air popping on top of the sludge, as if even oxygen couldn't wait to escape the dying waterway.

I sighed and settled onto my bucket for another boring day with my crotchety mentor, with only my dreams of the future to entertain me.

∞

That afternoon I reported to the police academy training center. Even though the bulk of my academy training was complete, there was a team-building exercise scheduled for my recruit class.

I'd been late getting off the boat, so I'd had to hightail it to make it in time. I was still pulling my hair back into the required bun as I walked in. Several of my classmates were already inside warming up and chatting about their experiences shadowing officers in the different departments.

No one greeted me when I walked in. I didn't take offense. They'd never greeted me during the academy classes, either. I went to an empty vinyl mat and started stretching.

A few of the guys nearby were chatting about their experiences on probationary duty. "I'm telling you, man, vice is where the action is." The speaker was a meathead named Bruce Batson. He was the kind of guy who joined the BPD because he wanted to get paid to swing his dick around.

"Nope," said Chuck Garza. "Busting Sinisters is way more fun. The Arcane division puts those freaks in their place."

I froze in the process of stretching my hamstring and shot the asshole a glare.

Chuck cleared his throat. "No offense, Prospero," he said in a resentful tone.

Sinister was a term Mundanes often used for

Adepts. A lot of people who weren't born with the ability to work magic were suspicious of those of us who could. The slur was offensive, but apologists said the slur came from the fact *sinister* meant "left" in Latin and all Adepts were left-handed. According to those people, anyone who took offense was just being overly sensitive. No doubt, the three men staring at me like they expected me to start crying fell into that category.

Instead of letting it upset me, I just went back to my stretching.

"Anyway," Bruce said in a patronizing tone, "it's too bad we have to serve time on patrol before we can do the exciting stuff."

A whistle blew, cutting off any chance of response. I jumped up from the mat and fell into line with the rest of my class. There were twenty of us in the group—sixteen men and four women. I was the only Adept in the bunch.

"All right, everyone. Today we're working on team building." The sergeant in charge of the drill was a hard-ass named Reams, who, according to gossip, was the first female to reach that rank in the department. She was six feet tall with a shock of spiky blond hair and permanently narrowed eyes. "You're going to divide into groups and cover each other as you work your way through an obstacle course filled with targets. Each group will have an appointed leader."

According to Reams, the goal of the lesson was to learn to work with a team in tactical situations. She counted off the teams. Naturally, I ended up with Batson and Garza, as well as two other meatheads. Next, Reams read off the names of the leaders. "Group three's leader is Prospero."

Male grumbles greeted the announcement. I ignored the pitch in my stomach at the news. I wasn't any happier than they were because I knew any mistakes on my part would be blamed on either my sex or my being a Lefty—or both. I pushed my shoulders back and girded myself for what I expected to be a frustrating afternoon.

"Split into your teams and head outside."

I turned toward the men, but they'd already started jogging toward the door, leaving me to follow. I cursed under my breath and double-timed it. I caught up with them just before the door, which I barely caught before it slammed in my face.

Once we were outside, I clapped my hands. "Okay, guys, round up." They ignored me and continued to the course. A field next to the training center held the obstacle course. Cargo nets were suspended from poles; walls without ropes to climb up, crawling obstacles, and other stations were spread across the field.

"Gather 'round," Reams shouted in a take-no-prisoners voice. Everyone complied immediately. I joined my wayward team, but none of them would step aside to allow me to stand beside them. "Each team will have to assist each other through the course. You'll all have paint guns, which members of the team will use to ward off attacks by training officers. The point is to work together and protect your team. Fastest time wins. Got it?"

After that, everyone broke out to strategize. My team circled up near the front of the course. "All right," Batson said, "Garza and—"

"Excuse me," I said. "I'm the leader of the exercise."

A shitty smile turned up his lips. He crossed his arms. "By all means." His tone was patronizing as hell, but I gritted my teeth and focused on the mission.

"All right," I said, "it looks like our most vulnerable obstacle will be the wall. We need two people to get over it first. I think we should station Batson at the bottom for cover and I'll help the others up."

Garza snorted. "Who's going to help you up?"

That's pretty much how the rest of the discussion went. I laid out a reasonable plan and one of the guys would contradict me. In the end we ran out of time when our group number was called.

I spent the next seventeen minutes and thirty-four seconds getting shoved out of the way or cursed at. The men on my team totally ignored my plans, choosing instead to bicker their way through the course.

In the end, we got last place.

"Thanks, Prospero," Batson said after the times were announced. "Way to lead out there."

"Excuse me?"

"I told you we shouldn't have taken that formation on the wet obstacle."

My mouth fell open. The maneuver he referenced had been his idea. But before I could call him on it, Batson stormed off. The others followed in his wake, but a few choice words blew back toward me on the breeze.

Later, Sergeant Reams found me sitting on a bench in the women's locker room. I had my clothes on, but couldn't find the energy to grab my bag and head home.

"Tough day, Prospero?" Reams wore a white tank top and green cargo pants. She leaned back against the lockers and grabbed the ends of the towel around her neck. I nodded and stared down at the blisters on my hands from climbing the obstacles. "The problem is you're trying too hard to make them like you."

I looked up. "Shouldn't a team get along?"

"Teamwork doesn't require friendship. It requires everyone to do their jobs." She pointed at me. "It requires trust and confidence that all members will hold their own when shit goes down. And no one, especially male cops, want a polite chick around when that happens."

"None of them wants a chick around, period," I grumbled.

"Hey," she said, "it's not easy but it can be

done. I've been on the force for twelve years now."

Being reminded that it was actually possible to rise up through the ranks helped me calm down a little. "How did you do it?"

She smiled, but there wasn't any warmth to be found there. "You want to fit in as a cop, you gotta make them forget you're a chick. The last thing a man wants to worry about when he's under fire is his ingrained instinct to protect a woman. You got to prove to them you can hold your own. Actually, more than that, you got to prove you could kick any of their asses."

I snorted. "That means I have to be better than all of them."

"Pretty much," she said. "But that's not all. If you're gonna succeed you have to figure which one you are."

"Which what?"

"A woman in law enforcement has three choices. You can be a dyke, a slut, or a bitch."

I blinked at her. "That's all? Those three?"

She nodded.

"Which one are you?" I had a guess, but I didn't want to assume and end up insulting her.

She laughed out loud. "You really need to work on your poker face, too, Prospero. It's no secret I'm a big old lesbian. My partner and I have been together for eight years. She's an EMT."

"Ah," I said. "Well, I'll leave that one to you

then."

She eyed me up and down. "Regardless of which option you choose, you'll still have to be faster, smarter, and a better shot than most of the men on the force in order to get noticed. And Lord help you if you ever cry or say one goddamned word about your period."

I hesitated. "Okay."

"I've seen your test scores and you've gotten high marks from the cops you've been shadowing. You'll do fine out there as long as you keep your head and don't let all the dick swinging distract you from the job."

"Understood." I can't say the talk made me feel better, but at least I had more insight in how to navigate the good-old-boy system than I'd had earlier. I blew out a breath and rose. "Thanks, Sarge."

"Hey, I heard you pulled river patrol duty."

I shrugged. "Yeah."

"How's Cap'n?" There was an amused fondness in her voice, as if she knew the old man well.

"Salty," I said. "He's forbidden me to speak."

A laugh escaped her lips. "That's Cap'n, all right. Don't let him give you too much shit. He's mostly bluster."

"Yeah, right," I said, thinking of the way he'd yelled at me that morning for accidentally dropping a line into the river.

"It's too bad," Ream said. "Back in the day he

was one of the top cops in the Cauldron."

I frowned. "Really?"

She nodded. "Back before the accident."

I frowned. "I thought he was put on river patrol duty because of his age."

She shook her head. "He took a bullet during a raid of the Arteries." *The Arteries* was the nickname for the abandoned subway tunnels that ran under the Cauldron. The project had been stopped before completion, and now the underground labyrinth was the domain of the Sanguinarian Coven and magic junkies looking to get their fix. Every cop in the city knew going down there was bad news. "It was about ten years ago," she continued. "Mayor decided to clean up the tunnels and sent a group down to round up the potion freaks. But I guess someone tipped off the Sangs. Cap'n took a bullet to the leg."

I blew out a breath at the thought of him lying injured and vulnerable in the rat-infested darkness.

"He was never the same after that. He was given a choice between a desk or river patrol."

I nodded. "I can't imagine Cap'n stuck behind a desk pushing paper."

"Right," she said, pushing off the lockers. "He seems to enjoy the patrol, but I don't think he ever recovered from the injury. The brass is just letting him serve out his time there until he can collect his pension."

Hearing the story made me more sympathetic

to the crotchety old guy. "Thanks for telling me."

She held up her hands. "Do yourself a favor and don't bring it up. Cap'n's a proud man."

I nodded. "Thanks for the advice, Sarge."

She tipped her chin. "Good luck, Prospero. You'll need it."

∞

I kicked in the front door of my apartment at seven that night. In my left hand, I held my keys and my duffel bag. In my right, a bucket of fried chicken. Behind me, Danny carried a bag of sides and drinks.

"So then David said that Ava told him that Riley wants to kick my butt," he said.

I put my stuff on the counter and turned to relieve him of his burdens. "Why?"

"I don't know. He tripped me on the playground this morning, too."

I frowned. "What did your day camp counselor say?"

"She told me I shouldn't antagonize him." He crossed his arms. "It's not fair. He tripped me."

I ruffled his hair. "Dealing with bullies is never fair, kiddo. Pass me some plates."

He sighed and turned to grab paper plates out of the tiny pantry beside the fridge. The entire kitchen had less space than the interior of my Jeep, so he bumped me as he moved past. "Here."

I took the plates and started filling them with food. "Look, I know you're frustrated, but if we get this new place, you can start at Pen's school." My best friend, Penelope Griffin, was a counselor at Meadowlake, the exclusive prep school Danny would start in the fall. The house I was hoping to rent wasn't in the same neighborhood, but it was only about fifteen minutes away as opposed to our current place, which was more like thirty without traffic.

He frowned. "But I want to go to middle school with my friends." Since it was summer, Danny was in a summer school program at the moment, but in the fall all of his friends would be going to a public middle school. I'd visited the place, and, even though it was far nicer than the prison parading as an education institution I'd attended, I wanted something better for my brother.

"You'll love it there," I said. We'd had this argument before, so I wasn't about to get into it again. "Let's eat!"

We took our plates to the living room and sat on the sofa, which would fold out to become my bed later. I flipped on the TV and we dug into our chicken. I was starving after a full day working on the boat, followed by the obstacle course debacle. Probably, I should have tried to get something more nutritious, but the chicken place was convenient and cheap, which pretty much checked every box on my must-have for life at the moment.

Danny flipped channels to find his favorite cartoons. I tuned it out and thought about Sergeant Reams's advice in the locker room. Truth was, as much as I wanted to deny that women were still required to fall into such narrow categories in order to succeed, I'd seen the dynamics at play over and over again at the academy and in the real world. So the question was, did I want to fight against the system or try to figure out how to work inside it?

It didn't take me much thinking to realize that the latter choice was better. In addition to being a woman, I also had the whole Adept thing working against me. A lot of cops were suspicious of people born with the ability to work magic. It went beyond the typical prejudices against Adepts because in police work, evidence gathered through Arcane means wasn't admissible in court. Still, a lot of Mundane cops saw their Adept counterparts as people who cheated the system to close cases. That's why most Adepts in law enforcement went the CSI route instead.

So really, I had no choice but to try to play within the boundaries of the system. When Reams referred to the dyke stereotype, she wasn't really talking about sexual preference so much as an attitude. But I wasn't sure I could butch it up convincingly enough to fit in. That left two choices: slut or bitch. While the slut thing sounded fun, I wasn't exactly a vixen. Nor was I willing to use sex to gain favor in the department. That meant that, by default, I was going to have to be the bitch.

If you asked any of my classmates from the academy, they'd probably tell you I already had it down pat. After growing up in one of the covens, I certainly understood how to employ swagger and a few choice words to shut down anyone who stepped up to me. Still, I wished it were okay not to have to play any role. I just wanted to be me.

I sighed and poked at my food.

"Hey, Katie?"

I looked over at my little brother. He had a smear of grease on his cheek, and his shaggy hair was in desperate need of a cut. "What's up?"

"Can I have your biscuit?"

"Sure."

He snatched it off my plate like an experienced pickpocket. I shook my head at him with a smile.

My phone rang over on the counter. I hopped up to grab it. "Turn down the volume, buddy." He grabbed the remote and pressed the button, but left a grease slick in his wake.

I grabbed the phone on the third ring.

"I'm trying to reach Kate Prospero," said a male voice.

"This is she."

"It's Bill Tanner," he said, "you applied to rent my house on Maple Avenue?"

"Oh, this is her." My stomach sank. In my

head I was already hearing him tell me we didn't get the place.

"I was just calling to let you know the place is yours."

"That's too bad—" I froze as his words sunk in. "Wait, we got it?"

"Baba recommended you highly."

"She did? I mean, that's great!" My right hand shot into the air and I did a little victory dance.

"When will you be able to move in?"

I paused and thought about it. My lease had been up a couple of months earlier so I was paying month-to-month until I could find a place. "Actually, I could move in as early as next weekend." Even as I said the words, I couldn't believe this was really happening.

"That'll be fine. I'll be out of town on a business trip, but I can leave the lease for you to sign and the keys with Baba."

"Perfect," I said. "I'm really excited. Thank you, Mr. Tanner."

"Don't thank me—thank Baba. She convinced me to give you a chance."

I paused. "That was generous of her."

He grunted. "Just pay your rent on time and don't break anything and we'll get along fine."

"Yes, sir," I said. "Thank you again."

I hung up the phone and spun around. "We got it!"

Danny looked up with his cheeks packed with biscuit. "Mmph?"

"The house near your new school. It's so great, Danny. You'll love it. There's a big tree and you'll have your very own room."

He swallowed and smacked his lips. "But I don't want to move schools."

I went to join him on the couch. "I know change is scary, but I really believe you'll be happy there. You'll get to see Pen every day."

He thought it over with a frown. "That'd be sort of cool, I guess."

"And the house has a big backyard."

His eyes lit up. "Can we get a dog?"

I hesitated. "Maybe." The dog discussion had been ongoing for the last year. I'd put him off this far by claiming our apartment was too small and no one was home all day to play with a dog. But now I'd just ruined that excuse. "Tell you what? Let's get moved in first and then we can talk about getting a pet."

"All right," he said. "But no fish. They're boring."

I ruffled his hair. "Deal."

∞

The next day Cap'n allowed me to leave my milk crate and join him in the pilothouse of the boat. That victory combined with the excitement of finding out we'd gotten the house made me ridiculously happy. I leaned forward with the binoculars at my eyes and a huge smile on my lips.

"What are you grinning about, girl?"

I lowered the binoculars and shot him an exasperated expression. "It's a beautiful day."

"Hmmph."

We were crawling through the waters farther from the mouth of the river. Here the factories and buildings of the city had given way to trees and farmland. The sun was warm, and a nice breeze drifted across the deck. A crane took flight from the surface of the water and flew a lazy circle overhead. This part of the river wasn't as polluted as the areas closer to Lake Erie, so wildlife was more plentiful.

"Don't know what's so beautiful about it," he grumped. He shifted to his right, taking weight off his left leg. Remembering what Sergeant Reams had said about him getting shot, I wondered if the movement had something to do with the old injury. "Get ready to tie up."

Excited to do an actual job, I jumped up and went to the starboard side, where the lines were neatly coiled. Cap'n angled the boat toward a dock. An old tin sign hung from a pole on the end of the dock. The placard had a picture of a kid sitting at the end of a dock, fishing. Under that were the words, EARL'S BAIT AND TACKLE.

When we came aside the dock, I jumped out to quickly tie up. "Tie her up tight," Cap'n called. He cut off the engine, and it took a second for my ears to adjust to the unaccustomed silence. I finished the knot he'd shown me and stood back to admire my handiwork. Cap'n climbed off the boat to inspect it. "Hmph."

With that, he turned and limped up the dock. With a grin on my face, I stared after him. Cap'n wasn't the kind of man to get real flowery with the accolades; the fact he hadn't yelled or found some small thing to nitpick about was his version of high praise.

He stopped at the end of the dock and turned. "Well? You comin'?"

I hopped to and sped to catch up with him. Stepping off the dock, we landed in a sort of open grassy area in front of an old building with a rusted tin roof. Fishing nets decorated the metal walls, and old dog snored in the shade.

Signs tacked to the walls advertised the store's offerings: night crawlers, red worms, wax worms, minnows, pike shiners, and maggots.

"Why are we here?" I asked.

"Seeing a man about a thing." His eyes sparkled with mischief that belied the no-nonsense tone. But before I could question him more, he reached around me. The old screen door screeched like a banshee. The dog wasn't impressed.

Inside, the bait shop smelled like rotten fish parts, old beer, and mold. I scrunched up my face, but Cap'n stilled and pulled a deep breath through his nose. "You ever fish, Prospero?"

"Of course not." I'd grown up in the Cauldron

with a single mother. My uncle Abe was the most likely person to take me fishing, but instead he'd taken me under his wing in the potion-cooking game.

He shook his head. "Kids these days aren't raised proper."

Considering I'd spent a lot of my childhood committing petty crimes and wanting to grow up to be the leader of my coven, I couldn't exactly argue with him. But I did make a mental note to be sure to take Danny fishing at some point. "What kind of project are you working on, exactly?"

At that moment a tarp-covered door to the shop's back room crinkled open. The man who emerged looked like an extra from *Deliverance*. His sun-weathered arms extended from a sleeveless T-shirt advertising a brand of motor oil. He wore a mesh cap on his head, and a toothpick jutted from his lips.

"Well, hell, Marty didn't know you was coming around today!" The man smiled, exposing sepia-colored teeth earned from years of smoking the cigarettes he pulled out of his pocket. He had the accent of a transplant from below the Mason-Dixon. I wasn't a linguistics expert, but I knew redneck when I heard it.

"Had a little time in my busy schedule," Cap'n said. For some reason, both men started cackling. Bored, I looked into a case of hooks and lures.

Once they sobered, the owner of the shop

nodded at me. "Who's this you got with ya?"

"This is Prospero," Cap'n said. "She's stuck with me for the week." His tone implied he considered himself the one who was stuck.

The owner lifted a cigarette to his lips and squinted as he lit the tip with a Zippo in his left hand. This told me he was most likely an Adept, which meant he'd been born with ability to turn Mundane ingredients into magic potions. Whether he actually used those talents was still up for debate. Not all Adepts chose to go through the training necessary to work magic. He exhaled the drag slowly as his gaze crawled over me like the maggots in his bait fridge.

I'd quit smoking a couple of years earlier, but, like most former smokers, I still craved the feel of smoke in my lungs. Seeing the cloud of nicotine emerging from under his mustache, though, turned my stomach.

"You must be Earl?" I said.

His eyes squinted. "How'd you know that?"

I pointed toward the door. "Sign outside."

He didn't crack a smile or relax his posture. Those two black eyes stayed on me as he spoke to Cap'n. "I got that stuff you wanted, Marty. Come on out back."

Cap'n turned to me. "I'll be right back."

I started to ask him what was going on, but he shot me a look that promised retribution if I got too nosy. With a sigh, I leaned a hip against the counter.

Without another word, the pair of men disappeared through the tarp. I heard their shoes on creaky wooden boards and low-toned discussion, but I couldn't make out any words. Pushing off the counter, I looked around the store. Several large fish were stuffed and mounted on the walls with brass plaques bragging each specimen's weight and the date it was caught. A drinks cooler along one wall offered six-packs of beer, sodas, and bottles of water. There were even a few shelves filled with snacks and convenience items someone might need on a fishing trip, like sunscreen and foam coolers.

In other words, it was really boring. I looked to the right and spied a cloudy window looking out on the shop's side yard. A rusted-out Chevy sat on cinder blocks in the tall weeds just beyond the wraparound porch.

The sound of a screen door closing echoed through the shop. An instant later Earl and Cap'n appeared on the porch. I quickly stepped behind a display shelf of koozies so they wouldn't know I was eavesdropping.

"These look real good, Earl," my temporary boss was saying.

"Glad you think so. You, uh, brought the payment?"

Cap'n reached into the inner pocket of his windbreaker and withdrew a thick envelope. I frowned. What the hell was going on? I'd spent enough time in the Cauldron to recognize a deal going down when I saw one. My conscience told me I was overreacting, but Cap'n was acting awfully suspicious about this entire visit.

I looked up in time to see the men shake hands and turn to come back inside. Jumping away from the window, I moved toward a display of fishing poles. The men emerged from behind the curtain.

"You ready, Prospero?"

I looked up as if he'd dragged me away from something very interesting. "Oh, sure."

Earl tipped the bill of his mesh cap. "Nice to meet you, ma'am." The way he said it, though, sounded anything but polite.

I forced a smile and nodded before following Cap'n out of the store. When we emerged from the screen door, the dog opened one eye and emitted a halfhearted growl. I jogged past it to catch up with my boss on the dock.

"What was all that about?"

He glanced out of the corner of his eye. "Nothing."

I laughed. "Didn't look like nothing."

He stilled and turned toward me. "You spying on me, girl?"

I raised my chin. "You were right next to the window."

"I don't know what you think you saw, but it's none of your damned business." With that, he turned and stalked across the dock's weathered boards.

"Hey," I called, following him. "I'm talking to you."

He waved a hand behind him, as if swatting off an annoying bug.

I walked over to where he was bending over the lines. "I might be a rookie, but I didn't fall off the turnip truck yesterday."

He paused and looked up under the brim of his BPD ball cap. "What?"

I put my hands on my hips. "What kind of potion was it?"

He eyed me for a couple of beats. Then he threw back his head and laughed.

"I don't see what's so funny about it." I crossed my arms.

He bent over and slapped his knees. "Hoo! I haven't laughed like that in weeks."

I cocked a brow.

The last of his chuckles subsided. "I wasn't buying a potion."

"What were you buying, then? Guns? Drugs?"

He clucked his tongue against the roof of his mouth, as if fighting off another round of laughter. "Lures."

I froze. "What?"

"Fishing lures." He pulled the package Earl had given him out of his windbreaker. I took it from him carefully and opened the flap. Inside, there was a plastic box filled with six little compartments. In each, there was a fishing hook decorated with colorful feathers and rubber worms. "They cost a king's ransom, too."

Heat crawled up my neck and up to my forehead. "Oh."

He snatched the box out of my hands. "Hmph."

I ran a hand through my hair and tried to collect my thoughts. "I don't get it. If you were just buying fishing stuff, why all the secrecy?"

He looked down at the dock. "Because I didn't want you to know."

"Know what? That you like to fish?"

He shook his head and squinted at me. "I'm taking an early retirement."

"Huh? Why is that a secret?"

"You don't get it. Where I come from, men work. They don't quit early just because something's hard."

"That's silly. You've been a cop—what? Twenty years?"

"Twenty-three. Don't change how I feel, though." He pointed down at his leg. "After my accident, I took the river patrol thinking it'd be a way to stay in the game. But I can't do it anymore."

"No one would blame you for that. I mean, I've only been with you a few days and I'm bored as hell."

He shot me a warning look.

"Sorry, but it's true. Anyway, there's no shame in taking an early retirement. But I don't get what the lures have to do with all this."

"They have to do with my plans." Two spots of red appeared on his cheeks. "Once I retire, I'm planning to head to Montana to open a fly-fishing business."

"That's cool," I lied. The idea of spending any amount of time in the wilds of Montana, thigh-deep in icy water trying to hook fish, was pretty close to my idea of hell. But I didn't mention that to him. Now that he'd opened up a little, I didn't want to ruin it by mocking his dream.

He nodded and looked at the river. Even thought we were upstream from the worst of the pollution, the water moved sluggishly, as if it simply had lost the will to flow. "Sure beats spending my time on this watery graveyard. Last time I tried to fish the Steel, all I got for my efforts was an old boot, a dead bird, and three bloated fish."

My mouth curled up. "Gross."

"No shit." He smiled at me. "You know, you might be all right after all, Prospero."

I tilted my head. "I'm a little offended you thought otherwise."

He shrugged. "Can't blame me. When they told me I was getting a rookie, that was bad enough. But then one of the boys from the academy warned me you had a chip on your shoulder about being an Adept and all."

I crossed my arms defensively. "I do not."

He quirked a gray brow at me. "Sure ya do, but it doesn't matter really. One thing I learned being a cop in this town is everyone's lugging around baggage. The trick is you can't let it trip you up when things really matter."

He put the box back in his windbreaker and lifted his face to the sky. Sucking in a lungful of the sun-drenched air, he smiled. "Anyway, I'd appreciate it if you didn't tell anyone else about my plan. I'm still waiting on the paperwork to go through."

I nodded. "Understood."

"All righty." He stepped onto the boat. "Untie that line and we'll shove off."

I smiled after the man. As it turned out, he wasn't so bad after all, either. "Aye, aye, Cap'n."

∞

The next day rain made traveling up and down the river a real pain in the ass. A yellow slicker covered my clothes, making me look like a large, annoyed banana. But the rain wasn't the only source of my frustration. I'd been on river patrol duty for four days. In that time, we'd done little more than float up and down the water. In fact, the only excitement we'd seen in the last few days was when a boater got himself caught on a sandbar and we'd had to tow him off.

I coiled the rope and threw the end on top of the pile. With a sigh, I lifted my head and looked up at the steel-gray clouds.

"What crawled up your rear end?" Cap'n said

in a gruff tone. He stood in the wheelhouse where the rain couldn't touch him.

"I'm just wondering when we'll do something exciting."

"Rookies," he mumbled, shaking his head. "Once you been on the force awhile, you'll learn to appreciate slow days."

I threw up my hands. "Do you honestly expect me to believe there aren't any crimes happening on this river?"

He shook his head. "You seen any?"

I stepped out of the rain, shaking the wetness from my hair. "How would we know? We haven't investigated anything."

The boat was crawling through the waters down near the abandoned steel factories. The old buildings loomed like metal giants along the shores. Instead of barges loaded with ore or metal girders, the water was filled with discarded trash, dead fish, and a thick oil slick.

"Look around you, girl. Nothing to investigate. This river died a long time ago."

I wanted to tell him that the river might have died, but we were still alive. But I knew I'd be skirting too close to talking about the reasons he'd been put on river patrol to begin with. Instead, I said, "I'm just saying that we should be doing more. I've seen plenty of boats tied up along the shore. Surely someone's committing a crime in one of them."

He chuckled. "So what? You want to just stop

FIRE WATER

at every boat and search them illegally in case
someone's breaking a law?"

His patronizing tone made me feel small. I
knew he saw me as an inexperienced rookie with
nothing useful to share. But I'd lived in Babylon
my whole life. I knew lots of criminals used the
river as a sort of bandit highway. My uncle Abe
had used small boats to ship potions to other
towns and also to receive illicit ingredients from
elsewhere.

"You might have decided to just waste the rest
of your time until retirement fishing and shooting
the shit with the guy at the bait shop, but I'm
here to learn about law enforcement."

He looked at me from underneath his bushy
eyebrows. I couldn't read his expression except to
know that he wasn't pleased. "You want to go
looking for trouble, maybe you should have
shadowed the Arcane squad or homicide."

I didn't mention that I'd done the more
exciting details, but they'd made me sit on the
sidelines, too. Instead, I plopped my ass onto my
bucket and shut my mouth. I couldn't risk
antagonizing him further and getting a bad report.

The only sounds were the water splashing
against the hull and the whirring of the boat's
motor. Up ahead, the steel girders of the
Bessemer Bridge spanned the river. Tires
bumping over the bridge's seams added a
rhythmic pulse to the river soundtrack.

Passing under the bridge meant we were

251

officially entering the Cauldron section of the river. The factories of earlier gave way to tenements and shantytowns along the river's edge. Here the water was even more polluted, as it was downriver from the industrial section.

The bucket was digging into me, so I rose to stretch. I pulled off the slicker and hung it from a hook. I leaned against the wall, looking out the window toward the shore. I'd grown up in the Cauldron, but I'd never had much chance to look at it from the water.

A tent city sat on the shoreline. A few people with stooped shoulders and the paleness that came with malnutrition moved in and out of the ramshackle shelters. A few trash cans dotted the slope, but no fires were lit that rainy day.

"You grew up around here?" Cap'n asked quietly. I glanced over and saw his gaze on the tent city, too.

I nodded and watched a woman carry a crying toddler into a drooping tent.

"Votary Coven?"

I glanced up quickly. "How did you—"

He nodded toward my left wrist. "The tattoo."

I looked down at the crowned Ouroboros coiled around my wrist. I'd gotten the tattoo on my sixteenth birthday, just after I'd become a made member of the coven. It had once been the proudest day of my life. But that accomplishment had been knocked down the list after I left the coven.

"Also your last name was a clue," he added. "You're related to Abraxas, right?"

My lips turned down into a frown. "His niece." I looked him in the eye, daring him to think less of me.

Instead, he simply nodded. "When did you leave the coven?"

"Five years ago."

"Why?"

"Someone I loved died." I sucked in a deep breath. "I couldn't stay after that."

I didn't mention that the person who died had been my mother, and the real reason I left was that she'd died from using one of the potions I'd cooked. It was easier to let people think grief chased me away instead of shame.

"So how does a girl who grew up in one of the most powerful covens in Babylon end up becoming a cop?"

I should have expected the question. Lord knew I'd been asked it dozens of times by classmates and superior officers. But I was tired of having to justify my reasons for trying to improve my life. "Why did you become a cop?" I asked, turning the table on the old man.

The corner of his mouth lifted. "I wanted to kick ass and take names."

I tried to imagine the old man in his younger years. "How'd that work out for you?"

He laughed and nodded down to his bum leg. "Worked out great…until it didn't."

"What happened?"

His gaze moved back toward the front of the boat. He fiddled with a couple of buttons before he responded. "Potion bust gone bad." He looked at me from the corner of his eye. "Sangs."

I looked away, but inside I wondered if I knew the person who'd put the bullet in my new boss. The Sangs were allies of the coven I'd grown up in, so chances were good. But I didn't have the courage to ask the shooter's identity. "I'm sorry."

"What for? You didn't pull the trigger." His tone was gruff. "Hell, you hadn't even gone through puberty when it happened."

I shrugged. "Just seemed like the right thing to say."

He chuckled. "Anyway, after the shooting, I guess the brass felt I wasn't fit for patrol anymore. Been on this floating hunk of junk ever since."

"Do you miss it?"

"What? Patrol?"

I nodded.

A wry smile tilted up the corner of his mouth. "I don't miss the bunions or having to hose vomit out of my car at the end of a shift. But, yeah, I miss it sometimes."

By that time, we were nearing the terminus where the river spilled into Lake Erie. Instead of continuing to ask him questions about what was obviously a sore subject, I quieted as he executed a turn to take the boat back upriver. I couldn't help but think about how different we were. He was a gruff veteran who couldn't wait to retire, and I was an ambitious rookie who was itching to hit the streets. To kick ass and take names, just as he'd once wanted to do.

How would I handle it if a bullet took me out of the game? I liked to think I'd be more resilient and bounce back quickly.

You let an injury take you out of a different game, my conscience whispered.

I tried to suppress that traitorous voice. My mother's death was different from Cap'n getting shot. It hadn't been an injury but a wake-up call. Cooking potions had always been a game to me. A challenge. But once my mother died from a potion I'd cooked, I realized that if I didn't leave she'd end up being the first of many, and I had a bad feeling eventually I'd be among the dead. Danny had been another factor in my decision to leave. I knew if we stayed he'd eventually be pulled into the game, too. And I couldn't stand the idea of my sweet little brother being tainted by the greed and violence of the potion racket.

"Prospero," Cap'n said.

I dragged myself out of the past and looked up at the man. He was looking out the window at something on the shore. "Yeah?"

"You see that?"

My gaze followed the finger he was pointing. We were passing the tent town again. Only this time, a motorboat that hadn't been there the first time we'd passed bobbed at a makeshift dock. A lanky man with stringy black hair who wore a stained wife beater with baggy jeans stood on the deck of the boat. His friend was onshore speaking to the woman I'd seen earlier with the toddler. This guy was short with a beer belly straining the seams of his black T-shirt. He had on shorts and flip-flops, which sank into the thick mud.

As we approached, we watched the shorter man hand something to the woman. She gave him something in return, which he quickly pocketed.

"What do you think?" Cap'n said.

I squinted at the men through a set of binoculars. The man on the boat had tattoos on his shoulders and arms. I could just make out the sickle-shaped alchemical symbol for lead on his left biceps. "My guess is Votary. But it's hard to tell. The coven's splintered since Uncle Abe was arrested. Could be self-starters."

Cap'n's face changed with the mention of the Votary Coven. "You're assuming they're selling potions."

I lowered the binoculars. "They sure as shit aren't selling her baby formula. Look at her. She's got the shakes and her skin is covered in lesions." Potion addicts usually had sores on their skin and irises ringed light blue. If I had to guess, the woman in question hadn't been freaking for too long; otherwise she'd have exhibited more extreme outward signs of addiction, such as oddly tinted skin or limb mutations.

"I'm not buying it," he said dismissively.

"Oh come on! A child could tell there's a potion deal going down."

He shook his head. "We don't have probable cause."

I pointed a finger at the trio. "We just watched the short guy sell her a potion. That's beyond probable cause."

Cap'n ignored me and steered the boat toward the center of the river. My mouth fell open as he throttled the engine. The pair on the speedboat turned to watch us speed by. The tall one even had the balls to wave at us.

"Turn this boat around so we can go question them," I demanded.

Cap'n shook his head. "It's getting late. Got to get you back to the dock to clock out for the day."

"Screw the clock. It won't take long."

He shook his head, stubborn as an ass.

I looked him in the eye. "You aren't retired yet."

The look he shot at me was as serious as a heart attack. "Drop it."

"But—"

The look he gave me said he was about two seconds away from reporting me for insubordination.

I shook my head and crossed my arms.

Leaving the wheelhouse, I went to the back of the boat to watch the criminals we'd just passed finish their transaction. My chest felt tight with frustration. How in the hell was I supposed to learn from this cop when he refused to investigate crimes?

∞

That night my best friend, Pen, knocked on my door about nine o'clock. I opened the door to find her holding a six-pack of beer. Pen wore jeans and a pale-pink shirt that made her brown skin glow. Her long, dark hair was pulled back into a ponytail. "Beer faery!"

I laughed. "Thank God. But we'll have to be quiet because Danny's sleeping."

She tiptoed across the threshold. "I was going to call, but I was already in the neighborhood so I took a chance."

I frowned. "Why were you in the neighborhood?" Pen lived in a nicer part of Babylon that didn't have a freakhead on every corner.

"T-Bone needed some help."

"Ah," I said. "He okay?" T-Bone was the new Arcane Anonymous member Pen sponsored. He had been struggling with his new sobriety, but he had been lucky to get an accredited psychologist like Pen as his sponsor.

She nodded. "Just a minor freakout," she said

dismissively. She'd been down the same road as T-Bone herself.

I cracked open a beer and handed it to her. "Sounds like we both need one of these." After she took it, I opened my own beer and took a healthy swig.

"Uh-oh? Trouble on the high seas?"

I leaned against the kitchen counter. "I don't know. This guy I'm assigned to is frustrating."

"How so?" She was standing on the other side of the counter and leaned her elbows on the surface.

"He's retiring soon, so he's avoiding doing any real police work. It's almost like he's afraid."

"Makes sense. If he's that close to freedom, he probably wants to avoid anything dangerous." Pen had made no bones about how much she worried about my new career path. Don't get me wrong, she supported my decision to become a cop, but I guess it made sense for her to worry that I might get hurt.

I shook my head. "Today we saw a potion deal going down on the river. I wanted to go intervene, but he refused."

"You're sure it was a deal?"

I nodded. "I think so. It had all the hallmarks of one. Regardless, it was shady enough looking that any cop worth his salt would have gone to question the parties involved."

"I take it you argued with his decision?" A knowing smile tilted her lips.

"Of course! I didn't join the BPD to cruise along the stinky river all day. I want to arrest people."

"You'll have plenty of opportunity to do that once you're sworn in. Why not enjoy the easy gig until that happens."

I sighed and shook my head. "I'm just ready to get started, you know?"

She reached across the counter and patted my hand. "You've worked so hard to get here, I'm sure it's frustrating to be on the verge of everything coming together."

"Yeah, you're right."

"Besides, you only have what? Two more days until this last detail is over? Then you'll be sworn in next week and can go kick all the ass you want."

I chuckled and took another sip. The best thing about having a psychologist for a best friend was always having access to the voice of reason.

Pen looked around the apartment and paused. "What's with all the boxes?"

"Did I not tell you?"

She shook her head.

"I got the house!"

Her eyes widened and a huge smile spread across her face. "Shut up!"

"We move next weekend." I'd been spending my evenings packing away our meager possessions. I still had a lot of work to do, but I'd already booked a rental trailer for the big move on Saturday. "Are you free this weekend?"

Her face morphed into a fake expression of reluctance. "I don't know, I've got a pretty busy social schedule." Dropping the act, she grinned. "Of course I'll help out."

"Cool!"

"Once you're settled, we can sit down and start on the application for Meadowlake, too. Since it's summer, the deadline has already passed to apply, but I can probably grease a few wheels to get him a space for the fall."

"That would be great, Pen. It would majorly suck if we moved and he couldn't get in."

She nodded. "I hear you. I've already talked to my friend in the admissions office. She said there should be no problem."

I looked down at the beer can in my hand. "Did you, uh, talk to the financial aid office, too?"

"I did."

I looked up. "And?" This entire plan hinged on the ability to get a discount on tuition; otherwise there was no way I could afford to send Danny there.

"They said there'd be no problem transferring the discount to Danny since I'm his aunt."

I snorted. "You told them he's your nephew?"

"African Americans can have white relatives." She laughed. "Besides, he's totally family." She smirked. "Just not by blood."

"Kate?" Danny called from the doorway of the bedroom.

"What's wrong, buddy?"

He yawned and wiped sleep from his eyes. When he opened them again he finally noticed Pen standing there. Without another word, he threw himself at her for a hug. She laughed and wrapped her arms around him. "It's good to see you too, dude."

I smiled at the pair. Even though Danny was about to start middle school, he sometimes forgot that and showed signs of the little kid he used to be.

"Pen and I were just talking about how much you're going to love Meadowlake," I said.

Danny pulled out of the hug with a frown. "I don't have any friends there."

Pen leaned down to look him in the eye. "You will," she promised. "There are lots of nice kids there. Plus, the school has really cool computers for all the students to use."

His eyes opened wide. "Really?"

She nodded. "You'll even be able to take a video game design class."

Danny looked at me like he couldn't believe his luck. "Awesome! My old school only had one computer and you couldn't play any games on it because it was so slow."

I smiled at him. "See? I told you."

"I guess I can give it a try," he said, trying to play it cool.

"Once you guys get moved into your new house, we can set up a time for you to take a tour of the school," Pen said. "You're going to love the library."

He frowned. "Books are lame."

I shook my head at him. "You know what else is lame? The fact you're up way past your bedtime."

"Aw man."

I pointed toward the bedroom. "See you in the morning."

He hugged Pen one more time before he dragged himself back to bed. Once the door was closed, Pen turned to me. "He's getting so big."

I nodded. "I had to buy him new shoes last week and he's already in the men's sizes."

She shook her head. "I remember when he wore light-up shoes with superheroes on them."

"It makes me feel old."

Pen laughed out loud, the sound coming from her belly and bursting forth like a song. "Girl, shut up. You're only twenty-two!"

At the ripe old age of twenty-seven, Pen considered me a baby. But while most twenty-two-year-olds were just finishing college, I'd graduated from the streets of the Cauldron, which made people like dogs—aging seven years for every one they survived. I knew what she meant, though. Sometimes I felt seriously old, but I really did have my whole life ahead of me, especially now that I was finally about to start a new chapter. Still, I couldn't let Pen's comment go unanswered. "Oh, that's right. I forgot about your advanced age. Maybe I should have a ramp installed in the new house for your old-person scooter."

She chuckled and took a swig of her beer. "For real, though. I feel like it's only good things for you from now on, Kate. The hardest years are behind you."

I held up my can for a toast. "To the future: May it be filled with good fortune and even better friends."

She tapped her can to mine. "And lots of super-hot dudes."

"Amen, sister."

∞

I arrived at the docks the next morning to find Cap'n already on the boat. "You're late," he snapped.

I glanced at my watch. I was five minutes early, but I let the comment slide. After the tension yesterday, I'd decided to take Pen's advice and try to just get my last two days on river patrol over with. "Good morning to you, too."

"Untie the lines."

I did as instructed as quickly and quietly as possible. Unlike the day before, the sun was shining and the sky was the kind of blue that only happened on a perfect summer day. A nice breeze was coming off Lake Erie, which chased away the worst of the river's funk.

"You done yet?" my grumpy partner said.

"All set," I said cheerfully.

For some reason my determination to be in good mood only made him grumpier. "What's got sunshine coming out of your ass today?"

I smiled sweetly. "Just looking forward to another day in your company, Cap'n."

He frowned and made a disgusted sound before turning to the wheel. For the next half hour, neither of us spoke as he navigated the boat through the river toward the Bessemer Bridge. I wasn't sure why he'd decided to head that direction since he seemed to prefer spending most of his day in the quieter and cleaner waters upriver. But I didn't dare ask him with the mood he was in. So I just sat on my bucket and enjoyed the sun on my face.

Soon the shadow of the Bessemer loomed overhead and we officially reentered the stretch of river along the Cauldron. I rose and went to the side of the boat. Sunlight didn't improve the look of the tent city. Instead of blending into the gray sky and mud, it stood out like a discarded old boot against the cheery blue sky and yellow light.

The good news was the motorboat was nowhere to be found. Maybe the potion dealers were off sunning themselves like the lizards they were.

With a sigh, I turned my back on the tent city and turned to see what Cap'n was doing. I was shocked to see him watching the tents as intently as I had been. For a man who'd refused to intervene the day before, he certainly looked interested in it.

"Your friends are gone." The words were spoken in a grudging tone, as if he was trying to budget his words to me.

I shrugged. "They're out there somewhere."

He nodded and turned his eyes back to the river. "Soon they'll be someone else's problem."

I frowned. "What do you mean?" I walked to the control panel and leaned against it so I could see his face.

"Paperwork went through. Tomorrow's my last day on the river, too."

My brows rose. "That was fast."

He glanced out the corner of his eye. "No sense dragging out the inevitable." For a man who'd just received news he would soon be free to do whatever he wanted, he didn't sound very optimistic.

"Why don't you sound happier?"

He shrugged but didn't respond. I let the matter drop because he clearly wasn't eager to talk about it. So with a sigh, I went back to my bucket. Only five more hours until I could cut loose for the day.

We didn't speak much for the next couple of hours. At noon, we docked at a filling station upriver and ate our sandwiches. I sat on the prow of the ship with my legs hanging over the water. He stayed under the covered area, as if he wanted to spend every possible moment he had left behind the wheel.

The water up in this part of the river was cleaner than farther down the waterway. Under my feet, little fish swam just beneath the surface. I threw in a couple of chunks of bread for them to fight over. I leaned my head back and looked up at a bird circling overhead, waiting for his chance to swoop down and get his own lunch.

Traffic near this section of the water was lighter, too. During the first fifteen minutes of the lunch break only two boats had floated by, both fishing boats headed farther upriver where the fish weren't poisonous.

It wasn't until I was done with my food and preparing to haul myself toward the back of the boat that the sound of a motor buzzed in my ears. I looked up to see the same speedboat we'd seen the day before zoom past, headed downriver. The driver of the boat was the lanky guy with long hair. His shorter partner wasn't with him. He sped past without looking in our direction.

I leaped off the deck and moved as fast as possible along the narrow edges of the boat to reach the back. "Did you see that?" I asked. "It was him."

Cap'n had been snoozing. At my raised voice,

he fell off the stool. "Tarnation, woman, you scared the piss out of me!"

I shook my head to dismiss his complaints. "The potion dealer from yesterday just sped past. We have to follow him."

Cap'n righted the cap on his head and took a deep breath before answering. "Why would we do that?"

I threw up my hands. "Because he's either on his way to deal potions or he's on his way to their hideout."

Cap'n tilted his head. "Hideout? You sound like Nancy Drew."

I crossed my arms. "Look, all I'm saying is we should follow him. See where he goes."

"I don't—"

"You got something better to do?" I said pointedly. "Perhaps finish your nap?"

His jaw set. "Cool your jets. I was just about to say that I don't think it's a bad idea."

I paused. "Really?"

He nodded.

"Well…fine then."

The corner of his mouth lifted. "You have to untie us first."

"Oh, right." I quickly untied the lines as Cap'n flipped the ignition. A roar sounded from the engine, and the water behind the boat boiled. I hopped back in. "Let's go!"

The boat took off from the dock at a surprising speed. In all my time on the craft,

Cap'n had kept the throttle low, but now we were really moving. The speed and the wind made me tighten my knuckles on the control panel. I glanced over at the old man, who had a determined look on his face.

"What made you suddenly change your mind?" I asked.

His mouth tightened into a determined line. "If I'm leaving, I'm going to do it in style."

I smiled with a mixture of adrenaline and relief. "Let's go kick some ass, Cap'n."

"Hell yeah!" He gunned the engine, and we took off like a shot through the water. The motorboat had a head start on us and we were entering a part of the river with more traffic, so we didn't have to worry about him seeing us trailing him.

We followed for about ten minutes before I saw the motorboat veer off the main river into a tributary that branched off to the right. Cap'n slowed our speed and followed at a distance. The water was narrower here, but luckily was still deep enough to accommodate our craft. "This is Breakneck Channel," Cap'n said. "It dead-ends about five miles from here."

Speaking of dead ends, if I thought the Steel River was polluted, it was nothing compared with the sludge we floated on now. "This water is totally stagnant," I said.

"No fresh water feeding into this stretch," he explained. "No real life at all." He nodded to the empty factories along the route, which had been closed down for years.

"Which means no customers along this route, either." That supported my second theory, which was that he was headed toward their hideout.

Up ahead, the motorboat pulled up next to a large boat that resembled a houseboat, but the miserable state it was in made it look more like a floating tenement. I pulled out my binoculars and took a look. The lanky dude made quick work of tying the smaller boat to the larger one and hopped aboard before disappearing inside the door on the two-level structure on the deck.

"There's an old mill road that runs long this stretch of water," Cap'n said. "I'm gonna drop anchor and we can continue on foot."

It was a good idea. It would be foolish to roar up next to the other boat. That kind of move would only invite gunfire. Approaching on foot gave us the added advantage of stealth so we'd know what we were up against.

Several minutes later, we ducked behind a stand of trees parallel with the houseboat. I'd brought the binoculars, but Cap'n confiscated them. "There are at least two men inside. Looks like they've got a lab set up, too."

He offered the glasses to me. When I looked through them, I saw Lanky and Shorty arguing next to a long table set up with a variety of glass tubes and flasks. "A floating lab," I said. "It's kind of brilliant."

"How you figure?"

I handed the binoculars back before answering. "Labs on dry land are tricky. Lots of wizards cook in their kitchens or bathrooms. But it's dangerous because if the fuzz puts pressure on you it's hard to move a lab. It can be done, but usually only in deep night. Putting a lab on a boat, though, gives you the ability to move it in broad daylight without anyone questioning you."

He nodded. "Sometimes I wonder what boys like that could accomplish if they put their ingenuity to good uses."

I smirked at him. "For a criminal it's not about getting ahead, it's about the thrill of getting away with it."

He shot me a look, but I ignored it. "How do you want to play this?"

He pursed his lips and looked over the boat with his naked eyes. "We gotta go in hard and fast so they don't have a chance to shove off. You enter through the aft and I'll come in stern side. We'll meet in the middle."

I nodded. "A little shock and awe, huh, Cap'n."

He grinned. "You look way too excited about this."

"Damned straight."

He nodded and his smile faded a little. "Just don't get shot."

"Yes, sir." I saluted him.

We split up, with each of us using the tree line

to disguise our approach. By the time I was even with the front of the boat, my heart was racing ahead of me. I palmed my Glock and swallowed to try to dispel some of the adrenaline. "You've got this," I whispered.

I glanced back and saw that Cap'n had taken position near the boat's stern. He nodded and counted down three, two, one.

I burst forward from the trees. Before I knew it, I was jumping from the shore onto the deck. My boots landed on the wood with a thud. Inside the boat, the argument cut off. "What the fuck was that?" a male voice yelled. I ducked against the wall of the structure where I couldn't be seen from inside. A loud noise came from the other end of the boat, signaling Cap'n was making his move. I took a deep breath and prepared to kick in the door next to me. But before I could, it flew open. Shorty ran out.

"BPD," I yelled. "Freeze, asshole!"

Shorty stumbled to a halt and turned slowly. His arms came up instantly. "Shit," he spat.

I moved toward him, but behind me the sound of a scuffle and male shouts reached my ears. I was torn between helping my partner and cuffing my own catch. Deciding quickly, I jumped toward Shorty. My hand was reaching back toward the cuffs on my belt when Cap'n shouted something. A loud thump echoed from inside the boathouse.

I grabbed Shorty's wrist and slapped a cuff on. Holding on to him, I turned to look into the boat.

Cap'n was lying on his side on the floor. He was way too still. "Fuck!"

Yanking Shorty's other hand behind his back, I made quick work of applying the second cuff. Using my foot, I swept his legs out from under him. He slammed onto his back. "Ow, bitch!"

"Stay," I commanded.

I ran back toward the house and barreled inside. "Cap'n!" Fear made me drop the nickname as I slid into a crouch next his body. He flopped over, cupping a hand on his bum knee.

"Go get him before he shoves off!"

"Are you okay?"

He nodded quickly. "Go!"

I jumped up, my breath panting in and out of my lungs, ran the length of the house, and burst through the second door. Something bit into the side of my face a split second before I heard the sound of a gun go off. My heart stopped and it was only instinct that made me duck. I put a hand to my face and realized the pain was from splinters of wood that broke off when the bullet hit the side of the building. My first thought was that I was okay. My second was that that had been way too close. My third, that this asshole meant business.

From my crouch, I crab-walked to the edge of the house. Lanky was on the port side of the boat, bent over the lines. A flash of metal told me he was cutting the rope.

Gripping the gun in my left hand tighter, I forced myself into a standing position. My pulse was thumping in my ears. My hand shook. I told myself it was adrenaline, but I knew that was a lie. I was scared. That bullet that almost hit my head marked the first time I'd been shot at. Sure, I'd seen plenty of guns and violence, but no one had ever tried to shoot me before. It's not like you see on TV. There's no commercial break for you to catch your breath. Right then, the boring days floating down the river suddenly sounded pretty good.

"Get your shit together, Prospero," I lectured myself. I sucked in a lungful of air and blew it out slowly. Marginally calmer now, I pivoted toward the side of the boat. "Put the knife down!"

I pointed the Glock at the guy. He froze for an instant and then raised his hands. A snake's smile spread his pale lips. "Too late, bitch."

As if on cue, the boat slowly began to float away from the shore. My shock only lasted a split second, but it was enough time for Lanky to dive through an open window on the side of the boat.

"Shit!" But before I could follow him back inside, a loud splash sounded from near the front of the ship. I looked over the edge in time to see Shorty bobbing up from under the water. Black sludge coated his face and bald head. He sputtered and his eyes went wide as it occurred to him that with his arms cuffed he couldn't swim.

"Help!" he shouted.

Realizing that sooner or later he'd realize he was only like eight feet from shore, I dismissed him in favor of going after his partner, who was inside the house with Cap'n.

More carefully this time, I approached the house. Crouching next to the door, I held my gun to my chest and turned my head to look inside. I couldn't see Cap'n, but I did see Lanky in front of the lab setup with his back to the door. He was cursing out loud and holding a gun pointed at Cap'n, who was sitting on the floor next to him.

I rose from my crouch and stormed the room. "Put down the gun and step away from the lab, sir," I said, projecting my voice. "You're under arrest."

Lanky turned sideways to look at me. He held my eyes and with deliberate movements knocked over a glass flask filled with bright green liquid. The movement tipped over the Bunsen burner, as well. My eye flared a split second before the chemical caught fire, which crawled rapidly over the table.

"Oh shit!" I yelled. "You stupid son of a bitch." Lanky had decided to destroy the lab in a vain effort to hide the evidence of his crimes.

Lanky cuffed Cap'n on the head with his gun on the way to the door. He burst through the back door and dove over the edge of the boat.

Stopping Lanky took a backseat to getting Cap'n and me off the boat before it blew. I ran past the rapidly spreading fire and knelt next to my partner. The blow on his head had rendered him unconscious. With strength born of fear, I grabbed Cap'n under his armpits and bodily pulled him toward the door. Loud popping noises signaled that fire was causing the tubes in the lab to burst. I tugged and cursed and yanked toward the door.

I was almost at the threshold when Cap'n snorted and shook himself violently. "Kate?"

"I need you to move!" I yelled. Tugging him by his collar, I pulled him the rest of the way out the door as the fire gave chase. Sweat poured down my forehead and trickled down my back. "Come on!"

He stumbled in my grasp toward the railing. I tried to urge him over the side, but he balked. "We'll be poisoned!"

"Better than getting flash-fried!" I bumped him with my hip. His arms windmilled for a moment before he tumbled ass-over-elbows into the sludge below. Once I was sure he bobbed back up and was out of the way, I sucked in a breath and jumped.

The water was cold despite the warm summer day, and thick; it was like jumping into a barrel of oil. I sputtered up toward the surface. I had to use my hands to swipe away the worst of the pollution to be able to look around. Cap'n was about five feet away, and judging by the slowness of his movements and the wincing frown on his face, his injuries were making it hard to paddle. I swam toward him instead of the shore. Grabbing him by the arm with my right hand, I stroked with all my might toward the shore. Behind us, the flaming houseboat was floating toward the main channel of the Steel River.

I labored toward the shore. Next to me, Cap'n was sputtering and cursing, but he didn't fight me. He kicked his good leg and moved his arm to help move us forward. It felt like it took forever to reach the side of the channel. My feet touched bottom and I used the leverage to help push Cap'n out of the water. He cleared the lip of dirt and fell onto his back, panting. I glanced over my shoulder one more time.

The flaming houseboat had come even with the police river cruiser, which was a good two hundred yards from where we were.

"Kate, come on." I looked up to see Cap'n leaning over and extending a hand toward me. "Quickly now."

I scrambled up out of the water with his help. My knees hit the shore and I spit to clear the taste of pollution and stagnant water from my lips. Commotion to my right caught my eye. I looked over and saw Lanky lying on the shore not fifty feet from us. Beyond him, in the distance, Shorty was struggling to regain his feet. They both looked like those ducks you see after an oil spill—covered in black oil and shell-shocked. I couldn't blame them, I felt pretty shitty myself.

I didn't hear the explosion. But I sure as hell

felt the wall of searing heat slam into my body. The concussion knocked me to the ground and made my hearing go fuzzy.

I don't know how long I stayed down. But when I opened my eyes, I couldn't see very well. They throbbed painfully, as if blood vessels had burst. I blinked a few times to try to clear my vision. A blurry mass lay to my left. Realizing it was Cap'n, I crawled toward him. Each movement felt like a new injury, but soon my fingers touched something solid. "Marty?" I couldn't hear myself. "Marty!"

A hand touched my face. I blinked again and my eyes finally cleared enough to see Cap'n's face in mine. He looked like hell with a gash bleeding freely from his head and his face streaked with sludge. "Are you okay?" he mouthed. He'd probably spoken out loud, but the only sound in my ears was high-pitched static.

I swallowed hard and nodded. Despite my confusion, I was pretty sure I didn't have any serious injuries. His face changed from relief to shock, and he pointed behind me.

I turned slowly. My mouth fell open.

The river was on fire.

∞

A week later I hefted a box from the trailer I'd rented to move our meager possessions into the new house. The move made the still-tender burns on my arms flare painfully. According to the doctor who'd treated my wounds, we were all extremely lucky to be alive—although I doubted Lanky and Shorty would have agreed with the sentiment.

Lanky, whose real name was Earnest Tuttle, and Shorty, aka Fred Higgins, had been arrested for conspiracy to distribute illegal Arcane substances, attempted murder of two police officers, destruction of public property, as well as couple of fuck-you charges courtesy of the EPA. It had only taken the fire department an hour to get the fire under control, but by that time the full brunt of the BPD and the media had descended on the river. After giving our initial statements, Cap'n and I had both been rushed off to the hospital. I hadn't seen him since.

On my way to the front door, I paused to watch Danny climb the tree in the side yard. With a determined look on his face, he scrambled his feet against the bark. A wave of some strong emotion rose in my chest. Pride mixed with hope and a lot of love.

This house was a dream realized. After years of struggling, I'd finally gotten us far away from the place where all our old nightmares lived. We could finally start building some semblance of a normal life.

A few days earlier I'd been officially sworn in as a full-time patrol officer with Danny and Pen looking on. I'd start walking my new beat on

Monday night. That morning, Danny and I had a date at Meadowlake for a tour.

"Hey, Kate!" he called. "Look at me!" He'd finally reached the tree's lowest branch and was hanging from it like a monkey.

I smiled. "I see you, buddy. Great job!"

I continued into the house and set the box filled with plates and cups on the kitchen counter. Pen was at the sink, looking out the front window with a smile. She'd been watching Danny, too. "I think he approves of the new digs."

I laughed. "I might never get him out of that tree."

She adjusted the rubber gloves and got back to scrubbing the sink with cleaner. "We should make the beds first. Where's the bedding?"

I ran my hand through my hair and nodded. "They're in one of these boxes somewhere."

She paused and stared at me for a moment. I tilted my head. "What?"

"I'm so happy for you, Katie. This place is perfect for you guys."

Warmth spread through my midsection. But before I could answer, a knock sounded at the door.

I walked over to open the screen and found Baba standing on the porch. "Hi, neighbor. I brought you a housewarming gift." She held out a platter of cookies.

I took the offering and held the door open with my hip so she could shuffle in. "You didn't have to do that." If anything, I owed her a gift for convincing the landlord to rent to us.

"Ah, it's nothing."

Pen came forward and introduced herself. The old woman shook her hand, but her gaze moved back and forth between us. "You didn't say you had a partner, Kate."

I frowned but then her meaning hit home. "Oh, no." A laugh escaped my lips. "Pen's my friend, Baba. We're not together."

She looked unconvinced. "Wouldn't be a problem if ya were. I'm hip."

Pen bit her bottom lip. "I'm just here to help Katie unpack."

"Hmph."

The awkward moment was interrupted by the sound of running feet a moment before Danny burst through the door. "Did someone say cookies?"

Baba smiled down at him. "You must be Danny."

He paused and looked up at the old woman. There was a streak of dirt on his cheek, and the starchy scent of boy sweat emanated from his skin. "Yes, ma'am," he said solemnly.

Baba's lips twitched, but she schooled her features. "My name is Baba. I'm your neighbor."

Danny looked her over, taking in the broomstick skirt, peasant blouse, and long gray hair. "You kinda look like a witch."

"Danny!" I called, mortified.

Baba threw back her head and cackled. "It's okay," she said to me. To Danny, she said, "As it happens, I am a witch."

His eyes widened. "What coven do you belong to?"

Baba shot me a curious look. "I'm a solitary witch. I grow herbs in my garden and use them to make homemade remedies and special teas."

When Danny still looked confused, I explained. "It's a different type of magic than what wizes use, kiddo." I didn't mention that Mundane magic was way weaker than the kinds Adepts created. No sense offending the woman after she'd done so much to help us.

"Actually," Baba said, "that's the other reason I came by. If you want, I could do a simple clearing ceremony to invite positive energy into the house."

"Um." I hesitated. "That's nice of you to offer, but I don't allow magic in my home."

The old woman froze. "But you're an Adept." She sounded suspicious, as if she thought I was pulling one over on her.

I crossed my arms. "When I left the covens, I swore off magic of all forms."

Baba's eyes narrowed and her mouth pursed to the right. "You're serious?"

When I nodded, she made a sound I couldn't interpret. "All right," she said slowly. "But I'm not talking about cooking any of them dirty potions or whatever. Just smudging the house with sage."

I shook my head. "It's still ceremonial magic. Like I said, I appreciate it, though."

"Suit yourself." She shrugged. She didn't sound offended so much as amused and a little patronizing. She turned to Danny. "Hey, kiddo, you want to come see my witch garden?"

He nodded eagerly.

The old woman looked to me. "That okay?"

I paused. I knew she was asking if hanging out in her garden broke my no-magic rule. It felt like a test. If I refused, she'd declare me one of those neurotic parents who kept their kids in a metaphorical bubble. "Go ahead," I said finally. Having the kiddo out of my hair for an hour or so would allow me to make some headway on unpacking. Plus, a garden full of herbs wasn't exactly the same as feeding him a magic potion. "Just be back by supper." I looked at Baba. "We're ordering pizza to celebrate. You want to join us?"

The woman's face cleared and she smiled. I passed the test. "Absolutely."

I wasn't sure what it was exactly, but she seemed relieved. Could it be that my witch neighbor had been feeling a little too solitary?

After the pair left hand in hand, Pen came to join me at the door to watch them go. "She's quite a character."

I blew out a breath. "Leave it to me to end up next to a witch."

Pen laughed. "There are worse sorts of neighbors."

Recalling the potion freaks who lived next door to us in the apartment, I nodded. "No shit."

For the next hour or so Pen and I worked together to get the basics of unpacking handled. We were just finishing making Danny's bed in the upstairs guest bedroom when a male voice echoed through the house. Pen shot me a curious look as I turned to go check out the new arrival.

When I walked into the living room, I found Cap'n limping through my new kitchen. He saw me and paused beside the table.

He leaned heavily on a cane, and his right arm was in a sling. "Looks like you're moving up in the world."

I laughed. "And you look like you got your ass kicked."

He shrugged. "Just a little run-in with some potion cooks."

I smiled at him. "How ya doing, Cap'n?"

"Didn't you hear? I'm officially a free man."

"Good for you."

He nodded. "All things considered, Chief gave me credit for the final day of my service." A dimple appeared in his cheek.

"How do you feel about that?" I asked carefully.

The corner of his mouth lifted. "Pretty damned good, actually. In addition to the pension, I'm looking at a nice little settlement for my injuries."

I nodded because I'd been contacted by my union rep about my own settlement. It would be enough to cover my medical bills, as well as help with the down payment on Meadowlake for Danny.

"Wow, Cap'n. It's like the end of an era."

He shifted on his good foot, as if to alleviate pain. "I'm leaving tomorrow for Montana."

My eyes widened. "So soon? I can't believe you're ready to walk away so fast."

"And never look back. This place has been home to every tragedy in my life, Kate. It's time for a fresh start."

"Fresh starts are good." I found it ironic that my own new beginning was leading me down the same path Cap'n was so eager to abandon.

"Don't look so sad, Prospero. A lot of good things happened here for me, too. And I wouldn't trade a single heartbreak or happiness. It's just time for me to close this chapter."

I nodded because emotion was clogging my throat. He limped forward.

"You got big things ahead of you. And I have no doubt you'll make your mark on this city." His lips twisted into a wry smile. "I mean, besides setting the river on fire."

A shocked laugh escaped my lips but I quickly sobered. "Keep in touch, okay?"

"I will as long as you promise not to step foot on a river patrol boat again."

Lips twitching, I saluted him. "Yes, sir."

Before I could brace myself, he pulled me into a gruff hug. When he pulled back, his eyes were red-rimmed and shiny with tears. "Take care of yourself, kid."

With that, Captain Smiley turned and limped away with his head held high. I watched him go with mixed emotions. On one hand, I was sad I'd probably never see him again. But on the other, I felt hopeful for both of us. He was about to embark on a new adventure that would allow him to get some much-needed rest and relaxation. And I was starting on a journey that would be neither relaxing nor restful, but would damned sure be an adventure.

"Kate?" Pen called from the door to Danny's bedroom. "You okay?"

I turned to look at my best friend. I couldn't blame her for her question, considering I had tears leaking from my eyes.

Just then the door banged open and Danny ran into the room. Baba followed him at a more leisurely pace, an indulgent grin on her lips. "Kate! I got these for you!" He had a clump of wilted daisies in his grimy fist.

I accepted the offering as he barreled into me for a hug. I wrapped my arms around the kid, inhaling the earthy aroma of dirt and the starchy sweat from his skin. And I knew that from that moment on I'd associate that scent with happiness.

"You know what?" I said, looking at Pen over his head. "I think we're gonna be way more than okay."

Pen crossed her arms and leaned against the doorjamb. "In that case, I think this calls for a celebration."

Danny pulled back. "Pizza!"

With that, my best friend, my little brother, my new neighbor, and I gathered in the kitchen to debate the merits of toppings. Looking around at all of them, I couldn't help but feel like the luckiest chick in the world. Even though Baba was a new addition to the group, she already felt like family. Granted, ours wasn't a traditional family, but considering I was an Adept who'd grown up in a dirty magic coven who had just been sworn in as a cop, I'd never done anything the normal way.

Yeah, I decided, our fortunes had definitely taken a turn for the better. From now on, I would leave the past where it belonged and focus on the future, which was looking brighter every day.

About the Author

USA Today bestselling author Jaye Wells is a former magazine editor whose award-winning urban fantasy novels have hit several bestseller lists. She holds an MFA in Writing Popular Fiction from Seton Hill University, and is a sought-after speaker on the craft of writing.

When she's not writing or teaching, she loves to travel to exotic locales, experiment in her kitchen like a mad scientist, and try things that scare her so she can write about them in her books. She lives in Texas.

To learn more about Jaye and her books, please visit www.jayewells.com.

68459454R00168

Made in the USA
San Bernardino, CA
03 February 2018